Blood Floe

Greenland Crime Series book #2

by Christoffer Petersen

Blood Floe

Published by Aarluuk Press

Copyright © Christoffer Petersen 2018

ISBN: 978-1-983242-83-0

www.christoffer-petersen.com

From the Midnight Sun,
from the Winter Night,
tomb-black,
no Word ...
We hardly knew
those that were lost

Author's translation from
NORDPOLEN
by
LUDVIG MYLIUS-ERICHSEN (1872-1907)

Fra Midnatssolen,
fra Vinternatten,
den gravkammer-sorte,
intet Bud ...
Vi kender jo knapt
dem, der blev borte

Chapter 1

Even in the unfathomable dark of the long polar winter there is always light – the moon reflecting on the surface of the sea ice, the green and white curtains of Northern Lights twisting across the black night sky, the stars, pinpricks of primordial light scrutinising the tiny villages and settlements clinging limpet-like to the barren west coast of Greenland. The houses add a warm, artificial light, casting yellow squares onto the snow through thick-paned windows, the tiny red lights of the radio mast glowing over the graveyard on the mountain's knee above the settlement of Inussuk, and a cigarette burning a bright orange, a smouldering flame just a few centimetres from the lips of the man wearing a headlamp, drifting the light slowly from left to right, as he searches the snowy black-sand beach for the skittish dog that shuns the harness.

Retired police constable David Maratse knew the dark side of all of Greenland. During his active years of service, he had seen more than enough evil deeds that even the blackest winter could not hide. Now, cigarette tucked into the gap between his teeth, he smoothed his bare hands over the webbing harness, pricking his thumb on the knot of waxed thread he had tied at the end of a stubborn line of stitching. The padding of the shoulder straps, as thick as his little finger, had been the trickiest to sew, the size and dimensions hard won as the sea ice thickened and the dog had wriggled and twisted between his knees, biting at the measuring tape each time the end flapped too close to its mouth. Other hunters he knew might have given up on the dog as a lost cause, been less patient, more insistent, but Maratse had time, and he owed the dog a debt of gratitude – the more he chased after it, the less he was bothered by the pain in his legs, the less he thought about the torturous root of it. He stuffed the harness into the cargo pocket of his insulated overalls, and sat on the reindeer skin tied to the battered thwarts of the wooden sledge with a zigzagging sealskin cord. The hollow-haired skin was stiff with cold; he could feel the ridges pressing into his buttocks.

He turned off the headlamp and finished his cigarette in the darkness. The dog would come to him, he reasoned, as it always did when he ignored it. He heard the soft crunch of snow beneath the dog's paws as it padded towards him, felt the smooth wet lick of its tongue on the back of his hand, and the cold of its nose as it pressed its face into the warmth of Maratse's neck. He ran his fingers through the dog's ice-beaded fur, up its chest, past strong shoulders, all the way to the collar around its neck.

"Hello Tinka," he said.

The dog skittered on the snow as Maratse stood up, turned it within his grasp and clamped its body between his knees. Maratse tugged the harness from his pocket, straightened it, and slipped the collar over the dog's neck. He bent the dog's front legs at the elbows and pushed one and then the other through the triangular loops of the harness. He had tied the stiff loop of cord to the end of the harness, and he gripped it now, just above the dog's tail, and let the dog wriggle out from between his legs. He tugged the dog down the snowy beach to the ice foot, and then onto the ice where the team was anchored. Maratse clipped the dog into the team traces with a small karabiner through the cord loop. The dog whined as he turned and walked back towards the beach for the sledge.

"Enough, Tinka."

Maratse took his time with the sledge, fiddling with the sledge bag, hanging it over the uprights at the rear, like a large envelope. He opened the canvas flap of the bag, making a last visual and physical check that he had everything he needed for the journey. The larger items of gear, the canvas tent, the collapsible metal stove, fuel, food, and clothes were tied to the front of the long, broad sledge, leaving just enough space for him to sit, at an angle, between the load and the uprights. The rifle he had bought from the gravedigger, Edvard, was holstered in a canvas bag tied to the sledge like a rifle slung from a cowboy's saddle. Maratse gripped the uprights and started to push the sledge towards the ice.

"Let me help you."

Maratse grunted a hello at Karl as his neighbour crunched through the snow and took one of the uprights and together they pushed the sledge up and over the ice foot.

"How's the dog?"

"Don't ask," said Maratse.

"That's her wriggling the lines into a bird's nest?"

"It is."

Karl laughed. "You're going to have a wonderful trip."

"You could come with me."

"I could," Karl said, as they turned the sledge to within a metre of the team anchored to the ice. He shooed the dogs away from the sledge runners with a clap of his hands as Maratse clipped a large karabiner through the thick rope loops forming a V between the curved tips at the front of the sledge.

"Then why don't you?" Maratse asked, as he walked towards the knot of lines tied through a chain frozen in the ice.

"Buuti is preparing for the meal on Thursday. I have to help."

"Hm."

"Don't forget you are invited." Karl kicked at the gear tied to Maratse's sledge.

"I won't."

"Good." Karl lit a cigarette, offered one to Maratse. "It's a long way to Svartenhuk, even with nine dogs."

"I know." Maratse gripped the bunch of lines in his fist. "Maybe I won't go so far. One, maybe two nights. A short run to the edge of the ice." He straightened his back. "You're worried?"

"*Naamik*," Karl said, "it's just, you're not a policeman anymore."

"I know."

Karl exhaled a cloud of smoke, and said, "You don't have to go looking for trouble."

"I don't." Maratse heaved the lines free of the ice.

"I think you do."

Maratse grunted and tugged the lines to the sledge. Karl moved to the back and gripped the uprights. The ice was smooth underfoot, and he pressed the toes of his boots against a ridge, squirming his foot into a solid stance as Maratse attached the dogs to the sledge.

"*Ah*," Maratse said, and the dogs settled for a moment, all but Tinka. He took a step on the ice and said *Ah*, louder this time, and Tinka lowered her head.

Maratse kept an eye on the dogs as he walked to the uprights. He nodded at Karl. "Tell Buuti I won't look for any trouble."

"It was me who said it. She thinks you are a hunter. I know you're still a policeman. Besides, I think trouble finds you."

"I'll be fine." Maratse finished his cigarette, gripped the uprights and nodded as Karl took a step back.

"See you on Thursday," Karl said, as he slapped Maratse on the back.

The lead dog was one of Edvard's old leaders, a small bitch called Spirit. Maratse hoped she would help him train Tinka. Spirit lifted her head, padded forwards to the end of the line, and pulled it tight. Maratse cast a quick glance at the rest of the team and gave the command to pull.

The team tugged at the lines and ran forwards; spread like a fan in front of the sledge, only Tinka was out of formation, until the momentum of the team tugged her into a position on the outside, to the left of the sledge. Maratse jogged behind the sledge, increased speed, and ran to the left, before leaping into the gap between the uprights and the gear. He settled his back against the sledge bag, found a comfortable position for his legs, and tugged the dog whip from where he had tucked it, beneath the cord that tied the tent to the sledge. He uncoiled the pencil-thick sealskin whip and let it run though his fingers into a five-metre line, trailing on the ice behind him. Maratse held the long wooden handle in a loose grip, and then cracked the end on the ice to the left of the dogs, smiling as Spirit pulled the team to the right. He adjusted course with another crack on the right, and then tucked the handle of the whip beneath the cord stretched tight over the reindeer skin. Maratse stretched his legs at an angle so that the heels of his boots tipped over the thwarts to one side. He rested his hands in his lap, clapping soft claps when he felt the team begin to dawdle, or when the scent of a fishing hole and the frozen innards scattered on the surface of the ice turned their heads.

The sunless twilight of mid-morning turned the black sky into a penitent grey. Maratse lowered his head, fumbled for the cigarettes in his chest pocket, and then patted the pocket smooth against the hook and loop closure, smiling at his thoughts.

"Piitalaat would say I smoke too much."

He scanned the thick layer of sea ice – an anomaly if one believed the climatologists – and turned his head to explore the shadows of the icebergs locked in place. One berg in particular, massive with three gnarled and twisted towers, would have been right at home in one of Maratse's beloved science fiction novels. He smiled at the thought of setting up camp, lighting the metal stove, and reading by lamplight, as the dogs curled up on the ice by the sledge. Retirement, he realised, held plenty of opportunities, and, despite the pain in his legs, he was still young, a year shy of forty.

The sledge bumped over a fissure in the ice, and Maratse spotted a narrow lead of open water, perhaps a metre wide. He clapped his hands, gave a few encouraging whistles and shouts, and the team picked up speed, dragging the sledge and Tinka onto the firm ice on the other side of the gap, with Spirit taking the lead. Maratse leaned back, proud of his team, content with his surroundings, at one with the environment. They passed the three-towered iceberg, and the shadows diminished as the high-peaked peninsula flattened to a long, thin finger of snow-clad granite stretching into the frozen sea. Maratse could see the smoke of condensing air on the open water, in the distance, at the brittle edge of the sea. He could see something else, too. A thin line pointing straight up, like a mast. He leaned forwards just as the dogs jolted the sledge with a spurt of curiosity to match his own. Maratse didn't chide or encourage the team. He let them run, as his own curiosity grew, and the shape of a broad hull anchored to the ice sharpened with each metre they sledged towards it.

A scent or tang of something had pricked the dogs' noses, and Spirit tugged them forwards. Had Maratse not been equally caught up in the shape on the horizon, he might have noticed that Tinka had shoved her way to run alongside the lead dog, bumping against Spirit's more experienced flank. Maratse shifted position, kneeling, and then standing on the sledge, one steady hand on the upright, as he leaned forwards.

There was a dark stain on the ice in front of the boat, a stripe of something, too thin to make out at this distance, but not altogether unfamiliar. Maratse slowed the team with long, slow commands to stop.

He pulled the whip handle free of the cord and timed his first step onto the ice, ignoring the pain in his legs as he ran to the head of the team and slowed them with casts of the whip, tracing figures of eight in the frigid air in front of the dogs. The team stopped, icicles hanging from their muzzles, as Maratse took hold of Spirit and smoothed his hand between the dog's eyes and through the cold fur of its jaw. He spotted a mountaineering axe buried deep in the ice and anchored the team to it before unhitching the sledge and studying the boat in front of him.

It was an aluminium-hulled ice-strengthened expedition yacht, one that Maratse had seen before, on the east coast, a long time ago. He recognised the broad hull, the generous glass cockpit of the bridge, and the name on the side: *Ophelia*.

The yacht was anchored to the ice with two lines, one axe holding down each line. The bow was embedded in the ice, sealed a few metres along each side of the hull. The sails were furled and stowed, the shrouds caked in rime ice, and the decks heavy with layers of old ice and new snow. It had been there several days, perhaps a week.

He turned away from the yacht and examined the stain on the ice. Two dark stripes of blood led away from the hull. The trail stopped a metre ahead of Maratse's sledge; either the blood was covered with fresh snow, or the wound had been staunched. He looked at the sharp semicircular peaks of Svartenhuk in the distance, and then back to the yacht. The blood was fresher than the ice on the deck. He took a step forwards, catching himself with the memory of Karl's last words. Maratse shook the thought away, and walked the last few metres to the hull. He found a short ladder on the starboard side, shouted a quick greeting in English, and climbed aboard.

There had been a snowfall in the night, and as he walked on the deck, Maratse stooped to brush snow from a narrow window, shaped like a long, thin teardrop. The interior of the yacht was lit with a weak light. Maratse pressed his nose to the plexiglas, squinted, and then took a breath as he noticed a body, a man, laying on the floor with a broad-handled knife protruding from his stomach.

Chapter 2

The air in the cabin was heavy with blood and faecal matter, the last physical act of the dying man. Maratse turned his face away from the steps leading from the deck to the cabin. He waited for a second and then descended into the cabin, one hand flat against the bulkhead. He scanned the dimly lit interior of the yacht. Two more crew, a man and a woman, both slim, were slumped at the table, the ends of the woman's long blonde hair playing over the bald head of the man. Another member of the crew, slumped on the floor, looked like she had slipped in the blood. There was blood on her forehead, crusted in her short black hair. Her arms were positioned at uncomfortable angles, as if the fall had surprised her. Maratse took another step inside the cabin, placed his hand on the top of the cabinet that jutted into the room, and then lifted it immediately to stare at the blood glued to his fingers and palm. He peered over the cabinet, tracing a generous spray of blood plastered against the wall. There, on the other side of the cabinet, was a fifth crew member, another woman, her feet pressed against the base of a shelf, her neck twisted, her head clamped in the corner by the oven. She had a knife in her throat, smaller than the one in the man's belly.

Maratse lifted a towel from a hook by the sink and wiped the pale palms of his weathered hands, the creases lined with blood. He stuffed the towel in the cargo pocket of his overalls and took a step forwards to peer at the woman lying on the floor, pausing as he lifted his foot; the floor was thick with blood. Maratse turned his attention to the crew slumped at and around the table. He retreated to the cabin steps, sat down, and fished inside his overalls to pull his mobile from an inside pocket.

"I need to talk to Simonsen," he said, when he got through to the Uummannaq police station.

"He's off-duty."

"All right," Maratse continued, "I want to report an incident."

"Your name?"

"David Maratse."

"Maratse? From Inussuk?"

"*Iiji.*"

"This is Danielsen."

"Danielsen, I'm on a yacht at the entrance to Uummannaq fjord. Two dead, three unconscious."

"Two dead? You're sure?"

Maratse glanced at the man with the knife in his belly, the fibres of his clothes stained black with blood. "I'm sure." He paused at the sound of Danielsen writing notes, the scratch of the nib just audible over the sound of Maratse's own breathing.

"What about the others?"

"Alive, I think."

"You can't check?"

"If I take one more step, I'll contaminate the crime scene."

"I need to know."

"Wait a minute."

Maratse placed his phone on the bottom step and moved towards the crew members at the table, choosing a route with the thinnest layer of blood. He turned the blonde woman's head and elicited a soft snort from her lips. A shiver ran through the man's arm as Maratse slipped his fingers inside his wrist to check for a pulse. The woman slumped on the floor with the head injury had the weakest pulse of them all. Maratse examined her head and took a closer look at the corner of the bench; a few of the woman's black hairs were clamped behind a fleck of wood, sealed with more blood. Maratse moved back to the steps and picked up his mobile.

"Two women and one man, all alive. One woman has a head injury."

"How's the ice?"

"Good along the coast. There's an open lead six kilometres north of Inussuk. You'll have to drive around."

"This is going to take a while. I need you to stay there. Can you do that?"

Maratse looked at the black-haired woman's head. "I can stay, but I need to treat the woman's injury, and check the others. I think they have been drugged."

"Do that. Just don't touch the dead."

Maratse flicked his gaze to the dead man and grunted an acknowledgment before ending the call. He slipped his phone into his pocket and took a moment to study the interior of the cabin. Beyond the blood and the bodies, there was little to suggest there had been a fight. There were empty glasses at one end of the table, brushed to one side by the elbows of the crew. Maratse looked but could not see a bottle of wine, beer, or any trace of the kind of spirits he imagined would be necessary to knock someone out.

Everything else inside the cabin was detailed and ordered. The phrase ship-shape came to Maratse's mind, confirmed by the laminated lists tacked to the walls. All he knew of the *Ophelia* was that it was a

German boat designed for use in the Polar Regions. There were framed photos screwed to the cabin walls showing the *Ophelia* locked in the ice as it wintered over in the Arctic and the Antarctic. The yacht was used to being moored in dark, isolated places.

On first inspection, the only items out of place that Maratse could see were the knives that were no longer on the magnet strip above the hotplates of the oven, but were now implanted in the bodies in front of him.

Unless they had stabbed themselves, Maratse could not see how they had been attacked. There was a curious lack of footprints of any kind in the blood on the cabin floor. He looked from the dead man to the dead woman, judged the distance to be little more than a metre, and then studied the clothes of the three survivors, all clean, apart from the spots of blood on the shoulder of the black-haired woman's fleece shirt. If they hadn't killed themselves, Maratse reasoned, then perhaps there was another crew member hiding somewhere on board.

Maratse looked behind the steps. The light was off. He saw a panel of switches and tried flicking them up and down. Either they didn't work, or the bulbs had been removed. Maratse glanced at the black-haired woman. Her wound could wait, he reasoned. He pressed his right hand on his hip, forgetting for a moment that he no longer carried a pistol. He took a step towards the door to his right. It was open, a hand's width.

"Hello?"

He waited for a response, took another step.

If someone was hiding inside the cabin, and if they had murdered the two crew members and incapacitated the others, then they would make short work of a single Greenlander in a confined space. Maratse shook the thought from his mind and took another step.

The howl of a dog tricked Maratse's heart into an extra beat. He waited until the other dogs had joined in, and walked to the door. He slapped it open with a flat palm, only to jump back as something black and heavy thumped to the floor of the sleeping quarters. Maratse peered into the gloom, stared at the shape on the floor, and then jumped again at the sound of a woman's voice.

"It's my bag," she said in English, "a duffel bag. It was on my bunk."

Maratse turned to look at the woman, who had her hand pressed to her head.

"It must have fallen."

"And them?" he said, and pointed past the woman, and into the galley. "Did they fall?"

The woman turned to look in the direction Maratse was pointing. Her hand fell from her head and she screamed. The scream changed pitch as the energy flooded from her body, and Maratse caught her as she lurched back towards the cabin.

"No," he said. "Don't look."

"Henrik," she said, the name pressed through the fingers she clamped over her mouth. She trembled in Maratse's grip as he lowered her to the floor.

"Let me look at your head." Maratse placed his hands either side of the woman's head, and turned her slightly towards the dim cabin lights.

"Is that a knife," she said, "in his stomach?"

"*Iiji.*"

"What?"

"Yes, it is a knife." Maratse let go, and said, "How many of you are onboard?" And, when she didn't answer, he asked, "How many crew?"

The woman turned to look at the man she called Henrik. Maratse stepped over her legs and squatted in front of her, blocking her view. He tilted his head to look in her eyes. They were glassy, pupils wide, unfocussed.

"What have you had to drink?"

"Drink? I don't know," she said.

"How many crew?" Maratse pressed his hand on her shoulder. "How many?"

"Six."

"Six? Total?"

"Yes."

"Stay here," he said, as he stepped over the woman, and walked the two steps to the cabin. There was a torch clipped to the bulkhead between the doors to the sleeping quarters. Maratse unclipped it and turned it on. He shone the beam inside the starboard sleeping area, stepping over the black duffel bag to shine the light into the corner. The beam caught on a reflective strip of a sail visible through the opening, cinched with a toggle and cord. He found more sails stowed in the corner of the second sleeping area, the torchlight reflecting off another patch of reflective tape.

Maratse walked past the woman and shone the torch beam over the other crew members, and then up the short flight of steps and into the galley. He stopped at the outer reach of the blood pooling on the deck. If he jumped he might land on the top step, or tumble down all three of them. Maratse snorted and stepped into the blood. He reached the top step with his second stride, crouched to point the torch beam deeper inside the yacht, towards the stern, and then descended the stairs. The shower was empty, as was the tiny toilet on the opposite side of the corridor. He found two more bunks on either side of the corridor, and a storage space in the bow with a crawl space and hatch, sealing the living area from the compartment used to store more gear. Maratse ducked out of the storage area and walked back to the generous living area. He climbed the steps, placed his foot within his own bloody footprint and crossed the galley to speak to the woman. He paused to look out of the cockpit window, and saw two pairs of lights in the distance, on the ice, beyond his sledge and dog team. He pictured Danielsen at the wheel of the police Toyota, and hoped that Simonsen was in a better mood than the last time they had met at a crime scene. Maratse unclipped a first aid kit from the bulkhead and carried it to the woman.

"Help is on the way," he said, as he crouched beside her. He opened the kit and tore open two alcohol swabs to clean the woman's wound.

"The police?"

"And ambulance."

"I think I know what happened," the woman said. Maratse stopped her with a shake of his head.

"I don't want to know."

"My friend is dead."

"The police are on their way. You can tell them."

"You're not a policeman?"

"*Eeqqi*," he said, and shook his head. "I'm retired."

"But you searched the boat."

"I found the boat."

"You helped."

"I reported it. The police are on their way."

"Why won't you help me?" She wiped her cheeks with the back of her hand.

"I've done all I can do," Maratse said. He stood up at the sound of car motors decelerating, and tyres slipping to a stop on the ice outside. "The police are here now, and the doctor. They will help you."

"You can't just leave," the woman said. She reached for his hand.

Maratse placed the torch on the floor beside the woman, and climbed the stairs onto the deck. He met Danielsen and the Italian doctor on their way inside.

"The chief is waiting for you on the ice," Danielsen said.

Maratse nodded and climbed over the railing and down the short ladder to the ice. He found Simonsen smoking beside his sledge and gear. Maratse's dogs shuffled within their traces, nosing the air, voicing their apprehension with low growls. Maratse shushed them and lit a cigarette of his own.

"Tell me, *Constable*," Simonsen said, as he exhaled a cloud of smoke. "How is it possible that you are always the first at the scene of a crime?"

"This is only my second since we have known each other."

"It's becoming a habit."

"It's a coincidence."

"It's suspicious, is what it is."

Maratse puffed at his cigarette and stuffed his hands inside his pockets. Simonsen squinted at him through another cloud of smoke.

"Do you want my report?"

"Report? You're a civilian."

"You called me *Constable*."

"Because you can't seem to let go. That's going to get you into trouble one of these days." Simonsen nodded at the yacht. "Perhaps it already has?"

Maratse tugged the towel from his cargo pocket,

and said, "I put my hand down on a surface. That's where you'll find my prints." He tossed the towel at Simonsen. "There's a set of my boot prints in the blood on the floor of the cockpit, next to the man with the kitchen knife in his stomach. You'll find more prints where I walked to check the rest of the yacht. The woman said there should be six crew members. Two are dead. Two are unconscious, drugged maybe, and there is a woman with a cut on her head. The last member of the crew, the sixth, is missing." Maratse flicked the butt of his cigarette onto the ice and took a step towards his dogs. "That was my *report*. You can call it what you like."

"Where are you going?"

Maratse pointed towards the mountains to the northeast. "Svartenhuk."

"Why?"

"Because that's where I was headed."

"When are you coming back?"

"Thursday. I have been invited to dinner."

"There and back in two days? Less now. You'll never make it."

Maratse reached down and unclipped the dogs from the ice axe. "We'll see," he said, and tugged the line to the sledge.

"You'll answer your phone?"

"Maybe." Maratse turned and watched as Simonsen strode across the ice to the yacht, smoke curling from his lungs, as Danielsen appeared on the deck and shouted for him to hurry. Then he clipped the dogs' traces through the karabiner and gave two soft clicks. Spirit herded the team into position as Maratse ran alongside the sledge. He leaped on board as Spirit and the team tightened the traces. Tinka ran alongside Spirit, and Maratse wondered if she was as eager to get away from the yacht as he was.

Chapter 3

The man dug his hands into the snow like spades. His fingers splayed inside snow-clad wool mitts, frozen, linking each digit with webs of wool and ice. They were bloody but they did not bleed. They were numb, like the man's mind. And yet, a single thought drove the man onwards, clawing at his conscience as he clawed at the snow. A day earlier, several hours past, he would no sooner have labelled himself a survivor than an explorer. Two equally foreign descriptions for what he actually was – a researcher, and what he actually did – research. Surviving, being a *survivor* was not mentioned in his job description, and he did not recall seeing it as a prerequisite for the *Ophelia Expedition*. He preferred the expedition's subtitle: *The Alfred Wegener Greenland Svartenhuk Expedition.* It confirmed his place on the team, and his position as *the* authority on all things related to Alfred Wegener. Those years of study, endless nights poring over heavy books in German and English, gloving-up to read musty journals from the field in the archives of the Alfred Wegener Institute in Bremerhaven, and removing his glasses to rub his eyes when searching the institute's online database, that *knowledge* had turned the researcher into a survivor. He *knew* there was a cabin, Wegener's cabin, at the base of the mountain upon which he crawled. The hunters they had approached were unusually reticent to provide details or to even acknowledge the existence of the cabin, but he *knew* it was there, and now he had to find it.

He crawled, bumping his knees on black-lichened rocks poking through the surface, scuffing the toes of his hiking boots, tearing at the elbows of his jacket. He wailed long curses, pressing and spitting the syllables through stubborn, bloodless lips. Between curses and on smooth stretches, he prayed, digging deep into his spiritual roots just as he dug deep into the snow, appealing to God, entreating God, and, when the straight-edged shadow of a roof captured his attention, he thanked God, thanked him for every spade of snow he shovelled beneath his body, as he crawled to the cabin door.

The wind, the tail end of a katabatic downdraught, nipped at the exposed flesh of his cheeks, flung more snow, spindrift, and ice, at his chin, his mouth, his blue lips, as he clawed at the handle of the door to the cabin.

"Please," he said, as the handle proved to be as stubborn as his lips. "Please."

It didn't budge, and the man dragged the stiff cuff of his winter mitts across his eyes to search the cabin for a window. He would smash it if he had to. But the only window was boarded, sealed from the outside, bear-proofing the cabin.

He pressed his head against the blistered flakes of green paint. He would die like this, on his knees, frozen in place like the foetal-cast victims of Pompeii. The cruellest of comparisons. Even in death, of all the thoughts his mind might conjure, it chose one of heat, lava-death, he could almost feel it on his cheeks, almost imagine the brittle patches of exposed lichen bubbling either side of the cabin, consuming him.

"No," he cried, and the survivor in him took over,

grasping that one straw of knowledge the man had overlooked. The cabin was designed to confound polar bears. He pushed his hands *up*, and the handle of the door moved as the heavy wooden door creaked. He pulled back and swung with the door until the snow shortened the intended arc and the man, the survivor, was presented with a gap the width of his head.

It was enough.

He rolled onto his side, bit at his lip, and shunted his body through the gap. The wind chased snow up his legs, blasting his face with one last gust of ice needles, and then he was inside. He slumped onto his back and choked, before he realised he was not choking but laughing.

He rolled onto his elbows, blinked at the ice coating his eyelashes, like staring through glue. He recognised the shape of the wood-burning stove, almost chuckled at the absurdity of burning wood in a land without trees, reassuring himself that in winter, the fire is always set. He laughed at the sight of the twists of newspaper and kindling inside the iron belly of the stove.

"There will be matches. A box with one or two matches sticking out, easy to grasp with cold fingers." Dieter forged thoughts that would keep him surviving.

There were three. Three matches sticking out of the box. He tugged his hand from the heavy woollen mitten, the ice beaded into the wool fibres rattled as he dropped it on the black timber floor. He struck the first match and stared at the flame.

He pressed the match to the paper. Too hard. The flame died. He lit the second match, watched as the flame curled around the paper, blackening the edges. He would have forgotten to add wood from the metal bucket to the fire if the pressing voice in his head hadn't reminded him, *"Light the kindling."*

Every bit of him was pleased, grateful, overwhelmed, and, when the heat from the stove pressed the cold towards the walls, and the flames lit the man's face, the shelves, the two small cots, and the stumpy wooden armchair that had long since sacrificed its legs for heat, he stood up, stumbled to the door, and closed it.

The man crouched in front of the stove, warming his hands as he did a visual inspection of the room, directing his gaze to the shelves for tins of food, the beds for blankets, the bucket for wood, and when that ran out then the cots for kindling. He stood up and plucked a rusty can of ravioli from the shelf, together with a metal can opener. He fiddled with it, and then sat down in front of the fire to warm his hands before working on the tin.

Needles of fire burst through his fingers as his flesh recalled what it was to be made of meat, muscle, sinew and bone, not wood and metal. The fibres were meant to flex, and the pain as they warmed sparked a string of anecdotes from his research. His recollection of those stories had secured him a place on the expedition, regardless of his quirks and social oddities, and now those same stories were coming true, and saving his life, as he opened the can and put it on top of the stove.

Again the voice in his head told him, *"You'll need water."*

He searched for a pan, found one, and filled it with snow from the drift inside the door.

Ice may have been better, but he didn't have ice, and he was not going outside, not now that he was warm. The man crossed his legs in front of the fire, feeding it as the ravioli bubbled and spat in the can on the flat stove top.

He wrapped his mitts around the can, dragged the armchair closer to the stove and listened to the air pop out of the snow inside the pan as he ate, pressing two bent fingers together like a spoon. With his feet flat on the floor, his knees were higher than the arms of the chair, and he smiled at his Lilliputian adventure as he assumed the role of Gulliver of the North. He preferred such thoughts and distractions, as his mind settled, and the voice of the survivor fell back into the shadows.

The dark recess of his mind, black like the polar sky, black like the lichen, black like lava – cooled and inert, but fertile.

A fertile, fervent mind.

The thought made him smile, but still he did not entertain more than a thought. Some things must be suppressed in order to survive.

He had to suppress them.

There were things to do.

He had found the cabin. By luck, perhaps, but he should not disregard his latent knowledge, his studies and education.

He licked his fingers and placed the can on the floor. It took some effort to get out of the chair, then he searched the cabin, beyond the shelves, above the stove, beneath the beds. He kneeled in front of a wooden crate turned on its side, its contents seemingly more valuable than the legs of the armchair. He smiled at the slim collection of mildewed magazines with stiff corners, curled and greasy as soap flakes. He flicked through a copy of National Geographic, placed it on the floor, covering it with a tattered Playboy magazine, a Danish Western novel – the pages held together by true grit and mould. Then he spotted something else, something that peaked the researcher's interest, flooding his body with warmth, the kind that needs no flame.

"What's this?" he whispered, as if words might damage the leather binding, crack the spine, or even chase the journal at the tips of his fingers into an Arctic mirage, a polar tease.

The leather felt real, pressing into the thick whorls of his skin as he ran a finger down the spine. He tugged the journal out of the crate, teasing the sides from the magazines that gripped it, reluctant to let go. He knew what he had found but suppressed his enthusiasm with the same resolve and detachment that he kept for his other thoughts, the darker ones, hidden in the shadows. He would deal with them when the time came, now he had to be the keen observer and objective appraiser of all things Arctic. This was not the first and only Arctic journal the man had held between his fingers. But if this was Alfred Wegener's missing journal, if this was the one he had been tasked to find, then it might be the last he held for a long time, perhaps forever. He knew it as soon as he opened the journal, the pages crackling at his touch, with a glance at the name, the date, and the location in which the journal was written, Alfred's journal, the missing one, the one that would crown the man's post-doctoral research, and secure a position – any position – at the institute of his choice.

"Anywhere in the world."

The thought reminded him of the satellite phone in his jacket pocket. He had done his job, shelter, warmth from the fire and food to eat, and, soon, he would have something to drink. The man ticked off Maslow's hierarchy of needs – now that the basics had been met he remembered *love*.

He pulled the phone from the deep chest pocket, and the collapsible antenna from the other. He removed the battery, warmed it in his fist, and placed the spare battery on top of the journal, and then moved it to one side. He stared at the journal for a few minutes until he judged the battery to be ready. He carried the antenna to the door, opened it a crack and planted the tiny tripod in the snow. He shut the door and screwed the lead into the satellite phone, inserted the battery, turned the unit on and waited for it to find a signal.

"I found it, Marlene," the man said, when his wife answered his call.

"Dieter?"

"I found it."

"It's late," Marlene said.

Dieter waited as his wife stifled a yawn, and then said, "I found Alfred Wegener's journal."

"You found the cabin?"

"Yes, and the journal."

"That's great, Baby, really. You must all be really pleased."

"What's that?"

"All of you must be pleased." Marlene raised her voice, and said, "There's a delay."

"I know."

"… others say?"

"What?"

"Oh, it's getting worse. What do the others say?"

"It's just me. I found it."

"I know you found it. I'm really pleased for you. But what about the others?"

"Others?"

"Oh, Baby, I'm too tired for this." Marlene

paused. "The others. The team. The crew. What do they think?"

"The crew?"

"Yes."

The man paced within the limits of the wire, and said, "It's just me. I found it."

"Are you alone?"

"Yes."

"Where are the rest of the team?"

"I don't know. I found the cabin."

Marlene sighed, and said, "Maybe it's the connection, but, it sounds like you are alone."

"Yes. I am."

"Where is the yacht?"

"In the ice. No," he said, "at the edge of the ice."

"And the crew? Are they on the yacht? Are they on *Ophelia*?"

"*Ophelia*? Maybe. I don't know."

"Why don't you know, Dieter?"

Dieter stared at the phone. He ran his hand through his hair, turned his head at the crackle and spit of the last piece of wood in the stove, and then looked at the phone again, frowning at the distant static chatter on the line. He pressed the phone to his ear, and said, "I found it."

"I know you did, baby." The line crackled with static, and Marlene paused. "I'm worried about you, Dieter."

"I'm all right," he said, and then, "I have to go. I love you."

Dieter stabbed the tip of a numb finger on a button and ended the call. He turned the phone off and removed the battery. He shook the snow from the antenna and coiled it beside the spare battery on the floor by the journal. He lined up the parts, cataloguing them in his mind, before adding another piece of wood to the fire, the last, more snow to the water warming in the pan, and then grabbed a blanket from the bed before settling in the armchair with the journal. He tugged a headlamp from his jacket, switched it on, and started to read.

The survivor in him had served many functions. He had helped Dieter find the cabin, helped him survive the cold, and now he would help him to suppress thoughts of the crew, to forget the yacht, for the moment at least. There were other, more important things, for Dieter to consider.

He remembered the briefing at the offices of the Berndt Media Group, once the final team had been assembled. He recalled the way Aleksander Berndt had stood, one hand in a trouser pocket, as he clicked a laser pointer with the other. Dieter had been fascinated with the man's passion, his fire, and, not least, his fortune.

"This area here," Berndt had said, circling a group of mountains on the map of Uummannaq fjord projected onto the screen, "is where we know Wegener was working, collecting data, before he died on Greenland's inland ice sheet. There should be a cabin. The locals know of it, but have, so far, been reluctant to confirm it. It is my belief," Berndt said, as he faced the team, "that they are tired of expeditions. There have been many of late, and we are just the latest in a long line. But, I also believe that if you find the cabin, establish a base of operations, and conduct a thorough investigation of the area, you will be rewarded."

"With what, exactly? It's a big area. We're going to need a little more information."

"Ah, Katharina," Berndt said, and smiled, "of

course, I might have known our captain would be the team sceptic."

"I'm not a sceptic, I'm a geologist. I've seen my fair share of granite. If I'm going to get excited about something, I'd like to know what to look for."

Dieter closed his eyes for a moment, letting the rustle of snow crystals against the wooden shutters, and the teasing of the wind at the corners of the bitumen roof, distract him from the memory of Berndt's briefing. He swapped his memory of the subtle scent of Berndt's expensive cologne for the rich Arctic odour of cold, damp mattresses, mildew, lichen, and earthy roots. He smoothed his fingers over the creased leather cover of the journal and thought about Berndt's reward.

"No-one knows for sure what secret is buried in those mountains," Berndt had said, "Wegener hid it well. The question is *why*?"

Dieter opened his eyes and turned the page. He was about to find out.

Chapter 4

Maratse screwed the last of the spikes into the ice and tightened the shrouds of the tent. He studied the thick clouds of snow hiding the peaks of Svartenhuk and decided that even if he hadn't stumbled across the yacht, the weather would have hidden anything worth hunting in the mountains. The light from his headlamp reflected on the snow caught within its beam as he fed the dogs with dried halibut heads from the sledge, working down the thin dog chain he had anchored to the ice. Once all the dogs had been fed, Maratse crawled inside the tent, tied the canvas door, and assembled the walls, base, door, and hotplate of the collapsible stove. He prised the tubular chimney sheets into one long length and pushed the end through a leather flap in the tent. He lit the stove and arranged his sleeping gear as water boiled in the small kettle Karl had given him. Maratse lay on a cot inside his sleeping bag, with an enamel mug of coffee by his side and a heavy paperback in his hands. He grumbled between the pages, squinting once or twice as he moved the book closer and then further away. After three more pages, he eased himself out of his sleeping bag and rooted through his pack for his glasses. A second cup of coffee later and he had given up reading altogether, as even the most engaging descriptions the science fiction author wrote couldn't compete with the images of the bloody interior of the yacht, and the two dead crew. He stoked the stove with enough fuel for an hour or more, and then turned off the light.

It didn't matter what he might have said to the woman in the yacht, and no matter how many times he told himself he didn't, the truth was that he did care.

"You can't just leave," she had said.

But he did, and yet it gnawed at him, just like the dogs scraping at the skin of the halibut, before they penetrated the cheeks to chew on the frozen white flesh beneath. When he closed his eyes he could see the two dead crew members, slumped in their respective corners of the yacht's living area. The first question that plagued him was not how, but *when* did they die? Were the victims drugged like the crew? How many glasses were on the table? Was it five or six?

Maratse stared at the reflection of the flames from the glass window in the stove door as they licked at the tent walls. Beyond the crackle of the wood in the stove, the swathes of snow cascading down the tent walls, and the dogs fidgeting on the ice, Maratse heard the distant sound of two vehicles retreating into the night, and pictured the police Toyota and the hospital Transit van that doubled as an ambulance, racing back to Uummannaq. Another world, his world, one he had left behind.

The small folding cot creaked as he turned on his side and closed his eyes. The dogs settled. Maratse forced himself to think of something else, anything else. He chose the image of Police Sergeant Petra *Piitalaat* Jensen, the wayward strands of her long black hair, soft dark cheeks, her smile, her pout, those lips. His final thought was of the thirteen years between them, not particularly remarkable in Greenland, but enough to push any further thoughts from his mind. Maratse felt the frame of his glasses cool against his cheeks, pulled them off, and listened to the snow trickling down the side of the tent.

The next morning he had to dig through the snow to find the ice screws. Everything took that bit longer, as he packed his gear, collapsed the tent, clipped the dogs into their traces, and anchored the team to a fresh bridge of ice he dug with the metal-edged ice staff before breakfast.

It was dark. The sun would not return for another two months.

Maratse secured everything to the sledge, hitched the dogs, and leaped on as Spirit tugged the team towards Inussuk. Their trip interrupted, they were going home. They passed the yacht two hours later. The dogs barely gave it a glance, while Maratse stared, remembering the stripes of blood on the ice outside the yacht. They would be covered with snow now, but the yacht would stay moored to the ice unless a storm and warm winds broke the sea ice into floes, causing the crime scene to drift away. He turned away from the yacht, clapped his hands, and leaned back against the sledge bag. He closed his eyes, felt his breath cool and bead on the light moustache above his lip, and cling to his eyelashes like tiny diamonds on each hair.

The dogs slowed at the open lead in the ice, the black water visible beneath a thin soupy coating of new ice. Not enough to stitch the two plates together, but plenty to fool Tinka as the dog tried to step onto it as Spirit leaped. Maratse clapped, encouraging the dogs with two quick calls, as they pulled the sledge and Tinka onto firmer footing, and the last stretch before home.

Maratse watched as Tinka fell in beside the lead dog, shaking the water from her legs with a strong lope to match the pace of the team.

"Lesson learned," Maratse said, and smiled as he settled on the sledge.

He didn't move again until the team bumped the sledge up and over the ice foot, flatter and easier to navigate at low tide. Maratse slowed the team with soft commands, stepped off the sledge and gripped the uprights, walking behind the team to the anchor points he shared with Karl and Edvard. Their dogs yipped and howled as Maratse sorted his team, marching one dog after another to its chain, throwing it a fish head from the blood and grime-spattered plastic crate hidden inside a wooden chest beside the dogs. Once the sledge was empty, and the dogs fed, Maratse slid the sledge up and onto the box so that the runners would not freeze in a sudden surface melt. It didn't matter quite so much on the beach as it did when the team was anchored on the ice, but Maratse took pleasure in doing things the same way every time. He carried his gear to his house, dumped it on the deck, and opened the door.

The phone started to ring before he had removed his boots. He kicked them off, shook and patted the snow from his overalls, and padded into the living room in his socks. He picked up the receiver on the sixth ring.

"Maratse," he said, and leaned against the windowsill.

"Constable David Maratse?"

Despite the static on the line, Maratse thought the English accent was strange. He waited for a moment, and said, "I'm retired."

"But you are David Maratse?" It was a man's voice, older than Maratse. Not Scandinavian.

"*Iiji.*"

"My name is Aleksander Berndt. The *Ophelia* is my boat." He paused, and said, "You are familiar with *Ophelia*?"

"I was on board, yes."

"That's right, the chief of police told me."

"Simonsen."

"Yes."

Maratse unzipped the front of his overalls, and said, "What do you want?"

"Well, I'm sure you can imagine this is a difficult time for the crew, and I feel that I'm very far away. I'm calling from Berlin. It's late here, and I just need to have some things in place, as quickly as possible, to solve this matter."

"What matter?"

"The *Ophelia*."

"Your boat?"

"Expedition yacht, yes. Rather an expensive asset. She is anchored to the ice, as I understand, without a crew. So I need your help."

"I'm not a sailor."

"I appreciate that, but you are a policeman."

"Was."

"That's right, you're retired. But I wonder if you would be interested in earning more money."

"Looking after your boat?"

"No, not quite. I have already arranged to have someone secure the boat in the event of a storm. But even if *Ophelia* is secure, the police will not release her before the case has been resolved, and that's what I want you to help me with."

"To solve the case?" Maratse shifted position. "I'm not interested."

"No? Not even for a substantial payment? I can make it worth your while, Constable."

"I'm retired."

"So you say, but I have an idea that you are not entirely satisfied with that particular arrangement. I understand you were hired earlier this year to help solve another case, one involving a missing girl? You see, Constable, I have done my homework, and I believe you are the very man I need to speed things along, and allow me to get my boat back to Germany, and my crew to their families. You understand, this is a very difficult time for everyone concerned. Greenland is so very far away, so remote, isolated. It would be a comfort for the families to know that the company, and me, are doing everything possible to help with the investigation and to speed it along the way to a happy conclusion."

"Happy?"

"Did I say that? I mean successful, of course."

Maratse turned at the sound of someone tramping up the steps to his house. He waved at Karl, nodding as his neighbour kicked the snow from his boots and opened the door.

"You've got company," Berndt said. "Perhaps I could call again, give you some time to make up your mind."

"I don't need more time, Mr Berndt. I cannot help you."

"Because you are retired?"

"Because I won't interfere with a police investigation."

"I didn't ask you to interfere, I asked you to investigate."

"It's the same thing, the minute I get involved."

Berndt sighed, and said, "I think you are making a mistake, Constable."

"Perhaps."

"But more than that, I think we both know that it will be difficult for you *not* to get involved. Hell, you are already involved; it was you who discovered *Ophelia* and the fate of her crew. Are you not in the least bit curious as to what happened? Don't you want to see the killer brought to justice? Is that why you retired? Because you stopped caring?"

"Goodbye, Mr Berndt."

"Wait…"

Maratse ended the call and looked at Karl. "I need a smoke," he said, and walked towards the door.

"I thought you were trying to quit?"

"I still am."

He pulled on his boots and followed Karl onto the deck. Snow squeaked like brittle rubber as they walked to the railing and lit a cigarette each. Maratse brushed at the snow on his wool sweater and zipped his overalls to just below his neck.

"How was your trip?" Karl asked.

"I think you know."

"We saw the police car and the ambulance from the window," he said, and pointed with the cigarette between his fingers. "We saw them come back too. You know Sammu? The local reporter?"

"*Iiji.*"

"He said someone was murdered on a yacht." Karl studied Maratse's face as he smoked. "He said you were the one who called the police."

"He's right, and so were you."

"How?"

"You said trouble seems to find me. It did."

"Again."

"*Iiji.*" Maratse finished his cigarette. "When are we eating?"

"Buuti says to come when you are ready. She told

the Danes to come at dinnertime."

Maratse laughed. "I bet that confused them."

"*Aap*," Karl said. "I told them to come at six."

"That was nice of you."

"I know." Karl squashed his cigarette against the metal lid of the rubbish bin attached to the railings. He dropped the butt inside. "See you later."

Maratse nodded and watched him leave.

The Danes – Sisse, her daughter, Nanna, and partner, Klara – lived in the house beside Maratse. The women were artists, working with natural materials washed up on the beach, or, in winter, discarded from ravens, foxes, and hunters. When Maratse arrived at Karl and Buuti's house, the Danes were already seated at the table, and Nanna was playing with a dog whip Karl had made for her with a short length of wood and a long piece of string. Sisse called out for Nanna to be careful as she swished the whip back and forth in front of Maratse as he walked into the lounge. Buuti hugged him and guided him to a seat next to Sisse.

"We watched you leave yesterday," Sisse said, curling her arm around her daughter as she bustled past with an imaginary team of dogs. She kissed Nanna on the head, prised the whip from her hand, and said something about playing again later, once they had eaten. Sisse turned back to Maratse. "Was that Tinka leading the team?"

"Spirit," Maratse said. "Tinka has to learn."

"But she is learning," said Klara, "from Spirit?"

"It's the best way."

"Nanna likes Tinka, don't you," Sisse said, and stroked Nanna's long blonde hair as she fidgeted on her seat.

"She smells of fish," Nanna said.

"Nanna likes to kiss the dogs," said Klara.

"Oh, she shouldn't do that," Buuti said, as she placed a heavy pot in the centre of the table. Maratse caught the smell of seal meat wrapped in bacon, a wonderful combination of meat from the sea and the store. "Sledge dogs are not pets. They are working dogs. You should teach her to throw stones at the dogs instead, to keep them away, stop them coming too close."

"Stones?" Klara said.

"She's right." Maratse nodded. He reached down to pick up Nanna's whip and studied it in the light. Nanna watched him as he turned it within his fingers. "If you stay away from the dogs, I'll teach you to use the whip."

"How about that, Nanna?" Sisse said. "Would you like that?"

Nanna nodded with a sharp dip of her chin. "Yes," she said.

"Yes, what?"

"Thank you."

Maratse put the whip on the floor, nodded when Karl offered them all a beer, and smiled as Buuti heaped a generous amount of meat and potatoes onto his plate. He let the Danes lead the conversation around the dinner table, as they always did at mealtimes. It was as if they didn't know how to enjoy their food without adding words to it. Maratse ate. He sipped at his beer, smiled at Nanna, and raised his eyebrows, *yes*, when Buuti offered him a second helping.

The seal meat settled in his stomach, and Maratse felt the beer relax him, to the point where he began to nod in the heat of the living room. Karl kicked him under the table, and Maratse lifted his head as he heard Sisse say his name.

"What's that?" he said.

"I said what are you going to do?"

"About what?"

"The yacht. We were just talking about it, and Karl said you had a call from the owner. He said he wants your help."

"*Iiji.*"

"So what will you do?"

Maratse turned the beer bottle within his fingers and shrugged. "I don't know," he said.

Chapter 5

Simonsen leaned against the door of the room designated as Uummannaq hospital's morgue. He tucked his hands inside the pockets of his police jacket and watched as the doctor examined the dead body of the Danish man from the yacht. A nurse followed the doctor around the shallow metal basin, nodding and making notes as the doctor spoke into the microphone hanging from a cord around her neck. The doctor, Elena Bianchi, was Italian, but had a better grasp of Greenlandic than Simonsen ever would, and a more than passable Danish, although her pronunciation of some of the odd Danish vowels made him smile. He twitched when she caught his eye, chiding himself at being caught watching her and not what she was doing.

"You realise we will need ice," she said, "for the bodies."

"I'll call the fish factory," Simonsen said.

"Of course, if you keep bringing me dead bodies, I might put in for a cold storage." Elena wiped her nose with her wrist. She gestured at the room, and said, "Although, I wouldn't know where to put it."

Simonsen stepped into the room and peered at the stomach wound. Cleaned of blood, it looked insignificant, hardly worthy of the moniker: *cause of death, knife wound to the stomach*. But he knew the wound had been deep, he had the knife in an evidence bag at the station.

"What about the woman?" Simonsen glanced over his shoulder and into the corridor behind him. He could just see the toes of the second body they had recovered from the yacht.

"When I'm done with him," Elena said. She tapped the nurse on the arm and said something in Greenlandic. Simonsen moved to one side as the nurse walked past him. He waited until the sound of her clogs, plastic heels tapping along the corridor, diminished, and then closed the door.

"There's not a lot I can do about the bodies, Elena," he said. "These two were imported."

"They are people, Torben; you make them sound like cars, or washing machines."

Simonsen scoffed, and said, "It would be easier if they were."

Elena caught his eye, and then flicked her gaze back to the dead man. "You don't mean that."

"I don't?"

"No. You care about these people."

"I care about the people of Uummannaq. I'm just concerned that we seem to be getting more than our fair share of imported crime."

"You're worried about your statistics?"

"I'm worried about Aqqa. We're only two. We need more officers."

"Then ask for them."

"It's not that simple." Simonsen sighed. "I could always retire."

"You're too young."

"I'll be fifty-nine in September."

Elena looked up. "A year older than me."

"Maratse retired at thirty-nine."

"He was invalided off the force. You know that. You of all people know he didn't choose to retire."

"But nobody talks about it."

Simonsen stepped back as Elena moved around the table to take a closer look at the dead man's ear. She took a swab and worked it inside the cavity, before holding it up to the light. She turned the swab in her fingers and clicked the microphone to record her observation of a pale green residue.

"What about Maratse's legs?" Simonsen asked. "I heard he came for a check-up recently."

"He was here at the beginning of November."

"And?"

Elena dropped the swab onto a paper dish. She peeled the gloves from her hands and dropped them into a yellow biological waste bin for incineration.

"That's confidential," she said, and moved to open the door.

Simonsen stepped to one side. "But is he getting better?"

"Yes," she said, and walked into the corridor. "Help me switch these two."

"I thought he was," Simonsen said, as he pushed the metal gurney that Elena guided through the door. She covered the man with a thick paper sheet, and then helped Simonsen roll the woman's body inside the makeshift morgue.

"The man died from his wound, but there's something odd inside his ear," Elena said. She clicked the brakes of the gurney with a quick jab of the toes of her clogs, and moved directly to peer inside the woman's ear. She tugged on another pair of gloves, found a swab, took a sample, and held it up to the light. "Nothing," she said.

"Nothing what?"

"I wondered," she said, as she inspected the dead woman's other ear, "if they had something similar in their ears."

"Like what?"

"Hamlet," she said, and waited for Simonsen to react. "Poison in the ear?"

"I prefer war movies."

"It's not a movie, it's a play. Set in Denmark?"

"I know what Hamlet is."

"Who," Elena said. "*Who* he is."

Simonsen lifted his hands, palms up, an apology. "Okay," he said, "tell me."

"The man showed no signs of struggling. Almost as if the knife was pushed into his stomach while he was sleeping."

"The rest of the crew were unconscious – drugged."

"Yes," Elena said, "Ketamine. It's also used to treat tinnitus by dripping it into the ear. We might not have a freezer for dead bodies, but our lab technician is a gift. She came in as soon as I called, took a blood sample, and identified Ketamine within an hour. I'm trying to convince her to extend her contract." She pointed at the swab. "I'll ask her to check if that is Ketamine too."

"What about her?" Simonsen pointed at the dead woman on the gurney.

"Cause of death – knife in the throat – but she has cuts here…" Elena lifted the woman's forearm and pointed at her wrist and the base of her palm. "And here." She lowered the woman's left arm and splayed the fingers of her right hand. "She fought. She wasn't drugged."

"The other member of the crew – the German woman," Simonsen said, and paused to check his notes, "Nele Schneider – said the dead woman was having an affair with…" He flicked to another page.

"Henrik Nielsen. The dead guy in the corridor." Simonsen tapped his ear, and said, "You don't just squirt something in someone's ear. You have to be pretty close." He paused. "Intimate. Kissing, maybe?"

"He would notice," Elena said. "But, in a passionate embrace? She could distract him." Elena held up her hands, and said, "I had better stop while I'm ahead. Just listen to me. It's not right for me to speculate. It's your case, Chief."

"And I rather wish it wasn't." Simonsen tucked his notebook inside his pocket, and jabbed a finger in the air above the ragged wound in the woman's neck. "So, she was murdered?"

"Yes."

"When can I talk to the crew?"

"They are under observation right now. The captain and the man are still a little groggy, but you can talk to Nele Schneider."

"Aqqa is outside the door," Simonsen said. "I'll have him move her to one of the offices upstairs, if that's all right with you?"

"It's fine. Take the office next to mine. It's empty." She sighed, "Another vacancy I'm trying to fill. If I can get a doctor for the month of December, I might be able to have a few days off over Christmas."

"When did you last have a holiday?"

"April."

Simonsen nodded at the dead body. "Thanks for your help." He turned to leave.

"You'll remember the ice?"

"I'll have Anton at the factory send someone over."

"Today?"

"As soon as they can," Simonsen said. He smiled and left the room.

The soft clap of clogs caught Simonsen's attention, and he thanked the nurse as they passed in the corridor. He tried to remember her name as he walked to the lift. Danielsen would know, he seemed to know all the young Greenlandic and Danish nurses who worked at the hospital. Simonsen found his young constable busy with his smartphone as he leaned against the wall between the two rooms where the crew of the *Ophelia* were being treated and observed.

"Busy?" Simonsen said. He stopped and adjusted his belt.

"Two of them are sleeping. The woman is pretending to. That's what the nurse said."

"Well, I want to talk to her. Bring her upstairs to the office next to Elena's."

"You don't want to talk to her here?"

"I don't want anyone listening in."

"Okay." Danielsen paused, and said, "What about Maratse?"

"What about him?"

"Do you want to talk to him?"

"Why? Do you think he did it?"

"*Naamik*, definitely not."

"Then why would I want to talk to him?"

Danielsen shrugged. "He's all right, Chief. He's one of us."

"He *was* one of us."

"You're always a policeman," Danielsen said.

"Tell that to Maratse." Simonsen turned to leave.

"Why don't you like him? Is it because of that Sirius woman?"

Simonsen took a breath and turned. He took a step closer to Danielsen, and said, "She cold-cocked us with a pistol downstairs. You do remember?"

"*Aap*," Danielsen said, and lowered his voice. "I won't forget that."

"Neither will I."

"But what has that got to do with Maratse?"

"He *helped* her, Danielsen. She was being held for the murder of her partner, and he helped her escape."

"We don't really know what happened."

"You're right," Simonsen said, and nodded. "We don't. But until we do, I don't trust him."

Danielsen tucked his phone into his pocket, and looked Simonsen in the eye. "Well, with respect, Chief, I do. And I hope you will too, one day."

"We'll see," Simonsen said. "Bring the girl upstairs."

The cleaners were using the lift when Simonsen pressed the button. He took the stairs instead. Thoughts of Maratse needled him as he climbed to the first floor of the hospital. He turned left, and walked through the waiting room, glancing at the tank of fish without breaking his stride. Tropical fish in Greenland. Each time he saw the tank, he entertained the idea of releasing the fish into the sea. If it wasn't for the pleasure it gave the kids when they came for an appointment, he would have done it already.

Simonsen opened the door to the spare office, sat down and placed his notebook on the desk. He closed his eyes for a moment, until he heard the squeak of Danielsen's rubber soles, and the flap of hospital slippers in the corridor. He stood up as Danielsen showed the young German woman into the room, and gestured for her to sit. Danielsen leaned against the wall at the back of the room beside a poster used to check patients' eyesight.

"How are you feeling?"

Nele glanced at Danielsen and then smoothed the hospital gown over her knees and zipped her fleece jacket to her neck. "It's cold," she said.

"I thought you'd be used to that?"

"It's warmer on *Ophelia*."

"But you have been outside. You skied with the rest of the crew to Svartenhuk, didn't you?"

Nele nodded.

"All of the crew?"

"The captain stayed on board *Ophelia*."

"So," Simonsen said, and checked his notes, "five of you skied across the sea ice, and hiked into the mountains?"

"Yes."

"But only four of you came back?"

"Dieter…"

"Dieter?"

"Our Wegener expert, Dieter Müller." Simonsen waited as a frown wrinkled Nele's brow. "We were having an affair. We argued on the mountain. He said he wanted to stay. I thought he did."

Simonsen made a note. "What do you mean?"

"Isn't it obvious?" Nele fidgeted in her seat. She held her arm across her chest and pinched her bottom lip between her finger and thumb, biting her nail between sentences. "He came back. Later," she said, "when he came back, later, he must have killed Henrik and Antje. He must have."

"How do you know he came back at all?"

"Who else could have killed them?"

"Why would he?"

"Because Henrik was sleeping with Antje."

"The dead woman."

"Yes."

"Because…" Nele bit her thumbnail. A thin line

of blood flooded beneath the nail, swelling onto the skin beneath. "Because Dieter was jealous."

Simonsen glanced at Danielsen. He looked at Nele, checked his notes, and then said, "I thought you were having an affair with Dieter?"

"I was."

"And did you know about Dieter and Antje?"

"Yes," she whispered.

"But you didn't kill them?"

"No," she said, and lifted her chin.

Simonsen frowned and made a note. A rumble of bubbles from the air unit in the fish tank drifted into the office, and Nele flicked her head towards the door.

"It's just the fish," Danielsen said. "It always does that."

Simonsen's chair creaked as he leaned back and studied the woman sitting on the opposite side of the desk. She started to bite her nail again, and, together with the fidgeting, she fitted the textbook description of nervous, traumatised victim. Except for her eyes. Simonsen scribbled a word in his notebook: *predatory*. Nele Schneider had the look of a predator.

"You were unconscious when David Maratse found you."

"We were drugged."

"How?"

Nele shrugged, and said, "The water? He must have spiked the drinks before we left the yacht."

"Who?"

"Dieter."

"But you said the captain was alone on the yacht."

"Yes." Nele lowered her hand to her lap, her shoulders sagged, and she twisted to look over her shoulder at Danielsen. Her mouth opened, and, Simonsen noted, her eyes softened. "It was the captain," she said, "*she* drugged us."

Simonsen said nothing. He put his pen on the desk beside his notebook, and folded his arms.

"You don't think so?" Nele said. "I wouldn't have thought it, if you hadn't suggested it."

"I didn't suggest anything," Simonsen said.

"But it makes sense, doesn't it?" Nele reached forwards and placed her hand on the edge of her desk, steadying herself, as her soft eyes lost their predatory sheen, and she tumbled onto the floor. Danielsen ran across the room to help her as Simonsen stood up.

"Back to her room, Chief?" he said, in Danish.

"Yes."

Simonsen watched as Danielsen helped the young German woman out of the office. He picked up his notebook and pen and followed them to the lift. Danielsen helped Nele with an arm around her slim waist. He nodded at Simonsen through the glass doors of the elevator, and sank from Simonsen's view.

Something about those eyes teased at Simonsen's mind as he processed the evidence, considered the angles, and wondered just how plausible it was that four of a six person crew were sexually involved, with more than one partner. Of course, they didn't need to have sex to become jealous, and jealousy – a Greenlandic trait – thrived in isolated communities, and what could be more isolated than the cramped confines of an expedition yacht?

Simonsen walked back to the waiting lounge. He sat down on the red-cushioned sofa. Designed to appeal to kids, he dwarfed it, with his knees on the same level as his chin. It was quiet. The bubbling rumble of the air filter, a soothing antidote to the jumbled thoughts he tried to corral. He tapped the corner of his notebook against his knee, and studied the fish. They wouldn't last very long in Arctic waters, and neither had the *Ophelia*'s crew. There was more to this. Perhaps the mystery residue on Elena's swab would provide more answers, that and an interview with the captain of the yacht. He wiped his hand across the stubble on his chin, thought about retirement, and thought once more of Maratse, pitching his tent somewhere on the ice. Perhaps it was time to discard what he didn't know, and accept the idea of having a retired police constable in the area.

He allowed himself a few seconds of contemplation as he chewed on the idea that Maratse was somehow involved with the murders, and then tossed it out, recognising it for what it was – just another malicious thought. There was currently enough malice in Uummannaq without Simonsen contributing to it.

The arms of the children's sofa crumpled beneath his weight as Simonsen pushed himself onto his feet. He took a last glance at the fish tank, and walked out of the waiting room.

Chapter 6

The sun does not rise in December, but, for the
hunters of Uummannaq, every day with good ice was
a gift not to be wasted. Maratse sat on the deck of his
house and watched three large teams sledge past the
settlement of Inussuk, as he smoked and drank his
first coffee of the morning. The full moon lit the ice,
the three teams, and the sledge carrying a fishing boat
to the edge of the ice. It wouldn't be the last team to
pass Inussuk, narwhal had been spotted south of
Upernavik in the north, heading south. Small narwhal
tusks could be sold for at least one thousand Danish
kroner, but it was the meat the Greenlanders valued
above all else, that and the *mattak* – the skin. Maratse
swallowed at the thought of a spicy curry with soft
squares of narwhal *mattak*, or a rich stew with large
chunks of dark narwhal meat; the preferred meat dish
for Christmas together with tiny Greenland potatoes
from the south. Maratse pictured Buuti badgering Karl
to sledge to the open sea in anticipation of the arrival
of the whales. Of course, Berndt's yacht was going to
provide a delicious topic of conversation for the
hunters camped at the edge of the ice, while they
searched for thin spumes of mist from the pods of
narwhal. Simonsen was going to have his hands full
protecting the crime scene.

Karl staggered down the steps from his house
with an armful of gear clutched to his chest and a
thermos flask tucked under his chin. He grinned at

Maratse as he crunched through the snow to his sledge. Maratse waved and watched as Edvard helped Karl with his gear and dogs. After half an hour, and a second cup of coffee, Karl climbed the steps and joined Maratse on his deck.

"You could come with us," he said, and lit a cigarette.

"I might come later."

"Have you decided what to do about the yacht?"

"Not yet." Maratse flicked the dregs of his coffee onto the snow. "I thought I would go to Uummannaq, talk to Simonsen, and see if he needs me to write a statement."

Karl nodded. "You can take my snowmobile. Buuti has the keys."

"Thanks, but I think I'll take the team."

"Sure." Karl finished his cigarette and shook hands with Maratse. "See you in a few days."

"Good hunting." Maratse waited until Karl and Edvard hooked the teams to their sledges and watched as the dogs pulled them up and over the ice foot. It really was a good year for ice, despite global warming. Everybody was happy, the settlements were connected, and the wind was light, the temperature a steady minus twenty degrees. The conditions were perfect.

Maratse kicked the snow from his boots and went inside his house. He left his boots at the door and dug deep in the pocket of his overalls to find his mobile. He wrinkled his nose at the battery icon flashing at the top of the screen, searched for Petra's number, and called her on the landline.

"Hello, Piitalaat," he said, as she answered.

"David."

Maratse pictured her smile, and waited as she

berated him for not calling for over a week. "I've been busy," he said, "training the dogs."

"Have you caught any fish?"

"*Eeqqi.*"

"Have you even put out a long line?"

"*Eeqqi.*"

"I thought that was the plan. To fish and hunt."

"I have been training the dogs."

"So you say, to fish and hunt." Petra laughed. "You're still struggling to adjust."

"You laughed."

"I'm sorry. I know it's hard."

"*Iiji.*" Maratse paused for a moment, and then said, "You heard about the yacht?"

"The double murder? Yes. They are sending two police officers from Ilulissat, and a detective from Nuuk."

"I called it in."

"You were the one who found it? The report said it was a hunter from Uummannaq area."

"Simonsen must have left my name out."

"He really doesn't like you, does he?"

"I suppose not."

Maratse fiddled with the lead connecting the handset to the receiver. Petra waited, and then said, "David, why did you call?"

"To talk to you."

"That's nice, I'm glad, but that's not all, is it?"

"The owner of the yacht called from Germany. He wants me to help speed up the investigation."

"That sounds familiar."

"It was different with Nivi, she was the first minister."

"She still is."

"I know."

"But you don't want to get involved?"

"I'm trying not to."

Maratse waited as Petra thought for a moment. He listened as she breathed and pictured her biting her bottom lip, or curling a loose strand of hair around her ear. When she spoke again, he could hear the change of tone in her voice, she had made a decision.

"Hunting isn't working out for you," she said. "You miss police work too much. It's not your fault you were given early retirement, David, but you can't change that. I think this is what you have to do, I mean, if people are going to pay you to help solve crimes, to assist the police, then I think you should do it."

"You do?"

"Yes."

"Hm." Maratse said, "I'll think about it. Thank you, Piitalaat."

"Promise me one thing."

"*Iiji?*"

"If you have to go to Germany, take me with you."

"I don't speak German."

"Exactly, but I do. You'll need a translator." Petra giggled and ended the call.

Maratse boiled the kettle and filled a thermos with fresh coffee. He changed clothes, tugged on his overalls, and pulled on his boots. He could feel the stiffness in his legs as he carried the thermos to his sledge. Sisse waved to him from the deck of her house.

"Are you going to the join the hunt?"

Maratse shook his head, and said, "I'm going to Uummannaq." He nodded at his sledge. "Do you want to come?"

"Really?"

"*Iiji.*"

"I'll check if Klara will look after Nanna.

"She can come too."

"Oh, she'll love that, thank you." Sisse opened the door, then paused to knock the snow from her boots. "We'll be five minutes," she said, and disappeared inside the house. Maratse walked on, pulled the sledge down off the wooden box, and pushed it a short distance away from his dogs.

Nanna was the first to come out of the house. She bounded down the steps with her toy whip in one hand and a tiny backpack in the other. She raced across the snow to where Maratse sat on his sledge. She jerked the whip back and forth in front of her, giggling as the knot at the end of the string slapped against Maratse's boots.

"Like this," he said, and took the whip from Nanna's hand. He showed her how to swish with her wrists, rather than snap with her arms. The string whip arced in front of him. "Now you." Maratse crouched behind Nanna and guided her hand. She giggled, swishing the whip in small arcs as her mother arrived and helped her put her arms through the backpack.

"We must do what David says, Nanna. All right?"

Nanna nodded and coiled the whip, as Maratse pushed the sledge towards his dogs.

"You remember what I said, Nanna?"

"Yes."

"Stay away from the dogs unless I'm with you."

"Even Tinka?"

"*Iiji,*" he said, "even Tinka."

Sisse wrapped her arms around Nanna, pulled her hat up for a second and kissed the top of her head. They watched as Maratse harnessed seven males and

Tinka, and attached them to the sledge. He nodded for Sisse and Nanna to sit at the back, where they could lean against the sledge bag. Maratse held the uprights, growling as the dogs fidgeted at the end of the traces.

"This is Tinka's first test as a lead dog," he said, with a glance at Nanna.

"Okay," she said, as Sisse clamped her arms around her daughter.

"Ready?"

"Yes."

Maratse gave the command to go and leaped onto the front of the sledge, he tugged the whip out from under the cords stretched tight across the reindeer skin, and guided the team with commands and snaps of the whip to the left and right. Tinka hesitated at the ice foot, the tide was in, and Maratse leaped off the sledge to help push them up and over the ridge of ice and onto the frozen surface of the sea. As soon as they were clear of the ice foot, Tinka settled into her position at the head of the team. Maratse had given her the longest of the ganglines, and she raced across the ice, a dog's length ahead of the males. Maratse grinned at Sisse and Nanna, tucked the handle of the whip under his thigh, and rested his palms in his lap. The moon was a creamy yellow in a deep polar-blue sky, and the only sound beyond the shush and grate of the runners, was the soft panting of the dogs and the creak of the sledge as it flexed within its bindings.

"What do you think, Nanna?" Sisse said, as she teased the hair from Nanna's brow and smoothed it under the lip of her hat.

"I like it."

Three sledges with large dog teams of more than fifteen dogs each raced past, heading towards the mouth of the fjord, and the open sea. Nanna waved at all of them as Maratse snapped the whip on the ice to help Tinka focus and to avoid a collision.

"Do sledges ever crash?" Sisse asked, as the last team raced past them and they sledged across the fjord to the icy coastline of the island of Uummannaq.

"*Iiji*," Maratse said. "I know of a *qallunaaq*, an Englishman, who crashed when a larger team enveloped his." Maratse slapped his palms together like crocodile jaws. "The hunter had to cut the lines to free the sledges. Just out there," he said, and pointed into the distance as he guided Tinka into the frozen harbour of Uummannaq, with a snap of the whip on the ice to her right. They sledged between the fishing trawlers and boats locked in the ice until Maratse slowed the team with soft commands and they approached a ramp of ice leading up to the road. A taxi waited for them to pass before driving down onto the ice.

"It's so busy," Sisse said, as Maratse secured his team to a metal loop sticking out of a rock between the fishing crates, pallets, and wooden boxes marking the winter storage areas for the hunters and fishermen. The dogs tethered here were in the older and younger brackets of the teams. More dogs were tethered to the ice, but the fastest dogs were racing for the sea, and Uummannaq bustled with the purchase of last-minute supplies. The majority of men and women that Maratse saw held a mobile to their ear, and the radios in the private cars and taxis were tuned to the local channel.

Nanna took a step closer to Tinka, only to be stopped by Maratse as he placed a gentle hand on her shoulder.

"What did we say, Nanna?"

"That I should stay away from the dogs."

"That's right."

"Even Tinka?" she asked, and looked up at Maratse.

"*Iiji*," he said, and pointed at the sledge. "Can you coil my whip?"

"Yes," she said, and ran to the sledge.

Nanna stumbled and fell over a clump of ice just as a snowmobile roared up the ice ramp and swerved to avoid her. The driver, a grizzled Dane with a bloody bandage wrapped around his hand, braked and yelled at Nanna. Maratse walked over to him.

"Hey," he said, "you're scaring the girl."

"She got in my way."

"You should have looked." Maratse waved his hand at the dogs and the people walking on the street. "You should be more careful."

The man let the snowmobile idle as he pulled the goggles from his face. He let them hang around his neck as he stared at Maratse; the whites of his eyes were red, flecked with venom.

"Do I know you?" the Dane said.

"My name is Maratse."

"The constable from Inussuk? Hah. I've heard of you." He beckoned Maratse closer with a bloody finger. "The Chief doesn't like you much, eh?"

Maratse wrinkled his nose in the wake of the man's breath, and said, "That's not your concern." He looked at the man's hand. "What happened to you?"

"Enthusiastic butchery," he said, and sneered. "Some of us have to work for a living."

"You're a hunter?"

"I hunt lots of things."

"David," Sisse called out, waving as he turned. She nodded at Nanna whose face was buried in her mother's jacket. "Perhaps we can go to the store?"

"I have to go," Maratse said. "What's your name?"

The man revved the engine and grinned. "That's for you to find out, *Constable*." He let go of the brake and spat before accelerating along the road to the right, past the café in the direction of the hospital. Maratse watched him all the way to the door, where the man parked and disappeared inside the hospital.

"He wasn't very nice," Sisse said, as she peeled Nanna from her body.

Maratse nodded. He looked at Nanna and forced a smile. "Shall we say hello to Tinka?"

"I thought you said I wasn't allowed?"

"When you're with me, you can," Maratse said, as he walked across to his team, and unclipped Tinka from the gangline. He held the dog by the harness and walked her over to Nanna. "Tinka is still young," he said, as Nanna stroked the fur around Tinka's ears. "The problem is," Maratse said to Sisse, "that children have the same height as the dogs. They look the dogs straight in the eye, and they don't back down. Sledge dogs are not pets; they're the closest thing to the wolf. They spend their life jockeying for position in the pack. They sometimes interpret a child's actions as a challenge, and when dogs are challenged, they either submit…"

"Or they fight," said Sisse. She nodded in the direction of the hospital, and said, "Not unlike men."

"Maybe," he said, and grinned.

Tinka strained within Maratse's grasp, and he pulled her back, as Nanna withdrew her hand, and Sisse helped her with her mittens. Maratse walked Tinka back to the team and clipped the line into the loop at the back of the harness.

"I think we'll go shopping," Sisse said. "Perhaps

we can meet in the café before going home?"

Maratse nodded. "I'll be at the hospital."

"Why? Are you going to find that horrible man?"

"No, I'm going to talk to the police." He pointed at the blue Toyota as it parked in front of the hospital.

"Does that mean you are going to take the job?"

"We'll see," he said, and waved as he walked along the road, crushing the stiff snowy tracks of the snowmobile beneath the soles of his boots.

Chapter 7

Constable Aqqa Danielsen stopped Maratse with a flat palm against his chest the moment he walked through the main entrance of Uummannaq hospital. He turned Maratse around and guided him back outside. Maratse lit a cigarette as Danielsen tugged a thin fleece hat from his pocket and smoothed it onto his head.

"Simonsen will kill you if he sees you in there," Danielsen said, as he took a cigarette from the packet in Maratse's hand.

"I doubt that."

"I don't." Danielsen took a long drag on the cigarette. "You weren't in the car with him. When we drove back from the yacht, I had to remind him we had people in the back. He ranted all the way to the hospital."

"Then what happened?"

"*Naamik*," Danielsen said and raised his hands. "Forget it. I can't tell you anything."

"You just told me that Simonsen was ranting all the way home."

"About you. I can't tell you anything about the investigation." He frowned at Maratse. "You're not working this case, are you? Privately?"

Maratse wrinkled his nose, *no*.

"Okay," Danielsen said. "One thing I can tell you is that one of the crew is missing, unaccounted for."

"There were patches of blood on the ice. Perhaps they were his?"

"How do you know it was a male?"

"A guess."

Danielsen squinted at Maratse though a cloud of smoke. He flicked the butt of his cigarette into the snow. "A male, mid-thirties, some kind of Alfred Wegener expert."

"Wegener?"

"Dead polar explorer. A German."

"The one who visited Svartenhuk?"

"*Aap.*"

"There's a cabin up there," Maratse said. "Why are you laughing?"

"It's the cabin they wanted to find."

"They?"

"The crew. They said no-one would tell them where it was. Who told you?"

"Karl."

Danielsen smiled. "He would know."

"So, they sailed here to find a cabin in Svartenhuk." Maratse finished his cigarette. "People don't kill each other because of a cabin. What were they really looking for?"

"They won't say. Simonsen has interviewed all of them, but no-one is talking."

"They were drugged, weren't they?"

"*Aap.*"

"By the missing man?"

Danielsen scuffed at the snow with the heel of his boot, and Maratse waited.

"Dieter Müller. That's his name. It's the only thing they do agree on."

"You need to find him."

"We're waiting for backup; they're sending a detective and couple of extra officers up from Nuuk. They're arriving on the flight to Qaarsut around lunchtime. We'll pick them up and drive to Svartenhuk."

"And the yacht?"

"We'll drop the detective off there, pick him up on the way back."

"But if the crew are at the station…"

"Being interviewed again by Simonsen."

"What are you doing here?"

Danielsen nodded at the window of the room closest to the nurses' office, three metres from where they stood. He pointed at a man sitting on the hospital bed. "Do you know who that is?"

Maratse recognised him as the man with the bloody hand on the snowmobile who he met earlier. "I just met him. I don't know his name."

"That's Axel Stein. He frightens the nurses, scares the children. He moved to Greenland before I was born. Drank his way through a job as a carpenter, beat more than one wife, and had his kids taken from him by the council, twice."

"The same kids?"

"Two lots. Two girls and one boy." Danielsen adjusted his belt. "He lives alone in a hunter's cabin with nothing but a bad smell and a bad temper. He hasn't hit anyone since he stopped drinking, but he hasn't been nice to anyone either. Never, as far as I can recall. He comes into town once a month for supplies, and to draw some cash from the bank. Most of the year, no-one sees him, and they forget how nasty he can be. He reminds them every chance he gets. I think he does it so he can keep living in the cabin. No-one will go there as long as he lives there."

"But he hasn't done anything criminal, recently?"

"Nothing on record since he beat his last wife, and that was fifteen years ago, maybe more."

"But he has a temper?"

"Wicked, according to Simonsen." Danielsen held out his hand and Maratse shook it. "I like you, Maratse. No matter what Simonsen says, you're all right. You helped in the search for Nivi Winther, and you pulled one of our own out of the water. You might not be a cop anymore, but you haven't stopped acting like one."

"That's what gets me into trouble."

"*Aap*," Danielsen said, and laughed. He nodded at the window. "I have to go. Stay out of Simonsen's way, and you'll be fine."

"What did I do wrong?" Maratse asked, as Danielsen reached the entrance.

"He thinks you were working with Fenna Brongaard, when she came through here. He thinks there are too many secrets in your past."

"And what do you think?"

"I try not to," Danielsen said. He smiled, and Maratse wondered if his smile was the real reason the nurses liked to have him around. "Look after yourself."

Maratse waited until Danielsen was inside the hospital. He looked through the window as the young police constable entered the examination room, saw the way the nurse touched his arm, and then watched as Danielsen gripped the front of his belt and weathered a string of abuses from her patient. He could hear the curses out on the street. Axel Stein, it seemed, was working on his reputation. The thought occurred to Maratse that the cut on the old man's arm could have come from a knife, either by accident or during a scuffle. He shook the thought from his mind, finding it difficult to imagine a reclusive Danish hunter travelling across the ice to rendezvous with a yacht and guide them into the mountains.

Of course, *that* actually did make sense.

Maratse tilted his head to one side and watched as Axel stood up and faced off with the young constable. To his credit, Danielsen didn't back down, and Maratse nodded. He was all right. He made up for his boss.

Maratse walked from the hospital to the café, ordered a coffee and a plate of twice-fried chips that had the consistency of greasy cardboard. They were just about edible with a generous sprinkling of salt. He had finished eating when Sisse walked in with Nanna. The little girl had a track of tears on each cheek and a stubborn twist to her lips.

"I'm sorry," Sisse said, "but do you think we could just go home? If you want to stay, I can maybe find a taxi. I heard they drive across the ice."

"We can go home," Maratse said.

"Thank you." Sisse frowned. "But you haven't bought anything."

"There's nothing I need. The shop in Inussuk has more than enough for me."

"No treats? Chocolate? Beer?"

"Buuti spoils me with her cooking," Maratse said, as he followed Sisse and Nanna out of the café, "and I smoke too much. They have run out of cigarettes in Inussuk and if I buy more in town I'll only smoke them." Maratse shrugged and pointed in the direction of the sledge. "That way."

"Are you trying to quit?"

"Maybe."

"That doesn't sound very convincing," Sisse said. She helped Nanna onto the sledge, and then sat down behind her. Maratse unhooked the dogs from the loop in the rock, attached them to the sledge, and led the team down the ice ramp. He jumped on when the dogs were on the sea ice and Tinka tugged the team into motion.

"I'm not convinced, but a friend thinks I should quit."

"The policewoman? Petra."

"*Iiji.*"

"She's very nice. Very pretty." Maratse glanced at Sisse. "Don't look at me like that. Klara and I are very happy together. Besides, Petra is only interested in men. That's easy to see."

Maratse pulled up his collar and shrank inside his overalls.

"Am I making you uncomfortable?"

"Hm," he said, and adjusted the hat on his head.

Sisse laughed. "I'm sorry, David. I let my mouth run away with my thoughts. I think your friend is very nice, and I like the way she looks at you."

"She's twenty-six."

"So?"

"I'm thirteen years older than she is."

"Why should that matter?"

"Hm."

Sisse leaned forwards to squeeze Maratse's shoulder. "You're not very good at this, are you?"

"*Eeqqi.*"

"Don't worry," she said, and let go. "You'll get better. We women like to think we are mysterious, but we're still human, most of the time." Sisse laughed and kissed Nanna on the top of her hat. "What about you? Are you happy again?" Nanna curled to one side and hid her face inside the crook of her mother's arm. "She wanted a doll, and I said she had too many already, and now she is pouting."

Maratse looked at Nanna, tried to catch her eye,

but she buried her face even deeper beneath her mother's arm. He looked up at the sound of a plane landing in Qaarsut, the icy landing strip south of Inussuk. It would be gone by the time they had passed the remote airport, but the helicopters would be shuttling all day between the mainland to the island. He remembered what Danielsen had said about backup arriving from down south, and replayed the conversation in his mind as Tinka led the team home. He chose not to tell Sisse anything more about Axel Stein, but thoughts of the man, and what he was capable of, nagged at Maratse until it was time to leap off the sledge and guide the team up the beach to the rest of the dogs. Nanna ran across the snow and up the stairs to her house. As soon as the dogs were tethered, watered, and fed, Sisse hugged Maratse.

"Thank you, David. It was very generous of you."

"Will she be all right?" Maratse said, as Nanna curled her tiny mittened hands around the handle and slammed the door.

"She'll be fine. It's my own fault. I've dragged her halfway around the world to satisfy my passion for art and nature. At some point, before she starts school, we'll settle somewhere, find a routine."

"Is that what you want?"

"Hell no," Sisse said, and laughed. "But, it will be good for her."

Maratse smiled as Sisse waved and followed her daughter's footsteps to the house. It was only when she had gone inside that he noticed the lights of his own house were lit, and a slim shadow passed the window.

Maratse coiled the whip and tucked it inside the wooden box with the rest of his sledging gear. He pulled the thermos flask from the sledge bag and poured a cold cup of coffee into the lid. He sipped at it as he stared at the shadow passing back and forth across the window. Maratse dumped the coffee onto the snow, lifted the sledge onto the box, and carried the thermos under his arm to his house. He paused at the top of the stairs, banged the snow from his boots, and opened the door.

The smell of perfumed soap pricked at his cold nose, as Maratse took off his boots, and shrugged out of his overalls. He left his thermos by the door and walked into the living room. The shadows had been cast by a young woman, her red hair twisted into a wet knot at the top of her head, with damp strands plastered to her pale and freckled shoulders. Maratse stared at her, as she danced around his living room, his towel knotted above her breasts; it barely covered her thighs. She hummed as she danced, and Maratse noticed the tiny buds pressed inside her ears, and the white cord leading to the iPhone in her left hand, the cord whipped up and down as she danced.

Maratse coughed, and the woman danced. He raised his voice, shouted hello, and waited as she stopped, opened her eyes, and pulled the buds from her ears. Maratse could hear the beat pumping out of the buds until the woman dialled down the volume with a swipe of her thumb.

"You're out of water," she said in English. "I think I drained the tank."

Maratse stared at her.

"Hello?" she said, and waved her hand in front of his face. "Did you hear what I said?"

"About the water?"

"Yes, about the water. Honestly, Daddy said you were smart."

"Your *daddy*?"

"My father, yes."

"And who is he?"

"Aleksander Berndt. He owns *Ophelia*."

"Is he here?"

"No," she said, and snorted, "obviously."

Maratse tapped his top pocket and walked to the door. He heard the woman say something. He ignored her. Maratse found his cigarettes in the pocket of his overalls, tugged on his boots and walked onto the deck.

He smoked as he wrestled with his thoughts. He flicked the cigarette into the snow, and lit a new one, turning his head as the woman appeared at the door. He half expected her to walk onto the deck in her towel, but her practical and slightly worn outdoor gear surprised and impressed him, fitting her like a glove. The way she wore her clothes suggested the cuts, tears, and repairs, were all her own. She plucked the cigarette from Maratse's mouth and held out her hand.

"My name is Therese," she said, and took a long drag on Maratse's cigarette.

"Therese Berndt?"

She shook her head. "Kleinschmidt. My family – my *ancestors* – probably spawned a whole bunch of Greenlanders. Mostly up north."

"Upernavik?"

"Right," she said, and blew smoke in Maratse's face. "But you're from the east."

"*Iiji*."

"See," she said, and held out Maratse's cigarette. He took it from her fingers. "I know these things. I've seen a lot of Greenland, and I studied you and your people. I have a PhD in Arctic Anthropology."

Maratse let the cigarette burn in his fingers as he listened, she took it back and leaned against the railing, making a show of studying him.

"Your skin is darker than most of the Greenlanders I have met. You're a little shorter than the average male, and," she said, and pointed the tip of the cigarette at Maratse, "your moustache is wispier than the men in Nuuk. No," she said, as she pressed her fingers to the hairs above his top lip, "you should keep it. It gives you that oriental look. Makes you look hot."

Maratse felt the colour rise to his cheeks, and he wondered if that was sweat beading on his brow.

"Why are you here?" he asked. His tongue was dry, and he had a sudden urge to get drunk on Edvard's home-brewed spirits.

Therese frowned. "I really thought you would be smarter than this." She stubbed the cigarette on the wooden railing and dropped it onto the deck. "Daddy hired you, and he sent me to boss you about." Therese ran the tip of her tongue around her teeth.

"What?"

"I'm kidding," she said. "I'm here to give you instructions, to help you investigate."

"But I haven't agreed to anything."

"Oh," she said, and took Maratse's arm, "I wouldn't worry about that. Come on inside, and I'll tell you what you need to know. We've got a busy day ahead of us tomorrow."

Chapter 8

Alfred Wegener was a genius. With each turn of the mildew-tinged thick pages of the journal, Dieter knew he had struck gold. What he had found was academic collateral, a currency that could change his fortunes and move Marlene and him from the slums of Berlin, to a more upmarket location, with, perhaps, room for a baby. These thoughts occupied Dieter as he read the journal in the breath-fogged light from his headlamp. He curled the tattered blankets around his shoulders, blew on the tips of his fingers, and drank lukewarm water straight from the pan. He had already sacrificed the book crate for heat, and, if he looked through the smoky glass window of the stove door, he would see the iron nails glowing bright between the flames.

Dieter pored over Wegener's field notes, nodding at the descriptions of the lichen, tapping the page when Wegener's itinerary fit with what he knew to be true. There was just one thing that eluded Dieter, something that made him read and reread the journal, tracing Wegener's words with the frost-nipped tips of his fingers. The late polar researcher seemed to have invented some kind of code, something about archaeology. But Wegener was a meteorologist, climatologist, and geologist by default, and Dieter could not recall an archaeologist being present on this particular expedition

"Unless I missed something," he said, his breath like dry ice, obscuring the pages of the journal in his lap.

Dieter put the book down and assembled the satellite phone. Once the antenna was set up, and the battery warmed and installed, Dieter punched in his home number. He stifled a yawn, ignored the fact that he couldn't remember having slept, and waited for Marlene to answer.

"Dieter?" she said. "I've been trying to call you. Why didn't you answer the phone?"

"I turned it off to save power," he said, and picked up the journal. "Marlene, I need you to find my notes. They should be in a box, by the side of my desk."

"We need to talk, Dieter. There was something posted online…"

"This is important."

"So is this." She paused. "A man came to the house. He asked all kinds of questions. He wanted to know if you had contacted me."

Dieter rested the journal in his lap and rubbed his face with his hand. He blinked sleep from his eyes – or perhaps it was ice crusting his eyelashes, his own breath sticking to the hairs on his skin.

"Marlene…"

"No," she said, "you have to listen. You are in the newspapers, even *Die Welt*. It says you are missing…"

"I'm not."

"…and that two of the crew are dead." Marlene stopped for a breath. "They were murdered, Dieter. Stabbed to death."

Dieter sighed. "Marlene, there is a box by my desk."

"Are you even listening to me? Stop talking about the box. I don't care about the box, and neither should you. They are looking for you. They want to find you, to question you."

"Who?"

"The police, the authorities. They have sent more police from the south of Greenland."

"To find me?"

"Yes."

Dieter let the phone drift from his ear. He almost dropped it. He turned the pages of the journal, found the first entry about something buried in the mountains. He pressed the phone to his ear, and said, "They know, Marlene."

"What do they know?"

"The secret. That's what they are looking for, not me."

"Secret? You're not making any sense."

"It's all right, my love…"

"No, it's not. Nothing is all right. This is not okay. You have to leave that cabin, go down to the ice and give yourself in to the police."

"But then they will find out the truth. I can't let that happen. It's my secret now."

"Dieter," Marlene said, her voice shook, and she bit back a sob. "You're not well. I see it now, just like the man said."

"What man?"

"The one I told you about. His name was Stefan. He said he was from Berndt Media. He looked like a soldier. He said he had some difficult news to tell me, that it was shocking. He asked if I wanted to call someone, or if there was someone he could call, to be with me."

"Why?"

"Because he said you were ill, that you were struggling, that the dark had affected you, that it had triggered a depression. He said the crew confirmed it, and that you had done… things. Terrible things."

"I left the yacht."

"How?"

"I had to get away, Marlene."

"When?"

"I didn't go back. I stayed on the mountain, after our first search."

"But when, Dieter? The man said you killed those people. That you were crazy, obsessed with finding something…"

"I did find something. It is wonderful, Marlene. It can change our lives."

"Our lives will never be the same again," she said. "That's what the man said. That's why he took your box of notes."

"What?"

"Your notes. He took all of them. He said it might help, if they could find evidence of your obsession, some kind of mental health problem, they might be able to help you."

"You gave him my notes?" Dieter's breath condensed in the cold glare of the lamp in gusts.

"I had to. Don't you see? I want to help you, Dieter. I want you to come home. I love you."

"My notes."

Dieter put the phone down on the floor and stood up. He twisted around the cabin, placing his hand on imaginary boxes, shuffling from one cot to the other, crouching to look beneath them, as if the wooden cot was his desk, the cabin his office, and the soft green glow of the Northern Lights were the streetlights on Admiralstraße, Berlin.

He heard Marlene's voice pleading from the satellite phone's tiny speaker. He whirled on it, and shouted, "Where are my notes, Marlene?"

She didn't answer. He kicked at the phone, ripping the cord for the antenna out of the unit. Marlene's soft cries slid into the corner of the cabin as the screen blinked with the symbol warning that the battery was low, drained like Marlene.

Dieter stopped in the middle of the cabin. With a short leap to either side, forwards or backwards, he could have touched the outer walls, slipped his nails behind the newspaper pasted to the old wood. Instead he clawed at his face, his blunt grimy nails drawing red lines on his cold, stiff cheeks, but no blood, it was too cold to bleed.

The satellite phone died with a single beep, and the screen went blank, and then black, like the night, as the clouds obscured the polar moon and the wind dropped to a reverent whisper.

Dieter gathered the journal into his hands, bound it with the sealskin thongs around the cover, tucked it into the inside pocket of his jacket and tugged the zip to a close. He collected the different parts of the satellite phone, hid the spare battery in the pocket closest to his body, coiled the antenna lead, and collapsed the tripod into one jacket pocket, the phone into another. Dieter looked at his mitts, studied the jagged holes and tears in the ragg wool weave. He zipped his jacket, pulled his fleece hat over his ears, and shaped his hood like a funnel to hide his face.

He crouched in front of the stove and waited for the fire to die.

As the flames flickered and the fiery nails began to cool, Dieter dug into the shadows, and glanced at the drift of snow spread, fan-shaped, inside the door. The still polar night enticed him out of the cabin, and he shut the door, smiling as he lifted the polar bear handle. The snow crunched beneath his boots, as he traced his route a few steps away from the cabin, turning his whole head, up, down, all around, staring through the funnel of his hood with his tunnel vision.

Was it really such a good idea to leave the shelter of the cabin?

"They are coming for me," was Dieter's answer, a new-found strength and determination, driving him on. Stronger than the will to survive, Dieter was driven to succeed, to discover Wegener's secret.

The lighter layers of windblown snow dusted the trail in Dieter's wake as he lifted his heels, picking his way down the glacial valley towards the sea ice. If they were looking for him, as Marlene suggested, Dieter convinced himself he knew why.

"They might have taken my notes," he said, his voice muffled, his warm breath tickling his nose, "but they don't know how to read them. They don't know what they are looking for."

Dieter pictured his bunk on board the *Ophelia*, and his duffel bag stowed beneath it. He thought about the thumb drive hidden between the bottom of the canvas bag and the stiff layer that gave the duffel bag its shape. His smile was hidden by the hood, but the astute observer might have noticed a lighter gait, a renewed purpose in his stride.

Conflicting thoughts countered his enthusiasm, thoughts that included the police, they could be armed. He was a wanted man. The police thought he was a murderer.

He shook the thoughts away. *"It won't be a problem."*

Only when he drew close to the ice at the foot of the mountain, where the sea lifted its frozen edges to the rhythm of the tide, did Dieter stop to pause, to think again. He stared in the direction he knew the *Ophelia* was anchored to the ice; he himself had dug one of the two ice axes into the frozen sea.

Dieter unzipped the funnel hood, pressed his head into the cool air and cinched the hood into a high collar. He took a step onto the ice foot, slid over its smooth edges, and stumbled onto the sea ice. He started walking, fascinated at the smooth, wide, empty path ahead of him, interspersed as it was with the occasional iceberg. He sought out the familiar bergs they had used as waypoints from the yacht to the mountains, found them, altered course, and concentrated on walking at an efficient speed through the night, his second night without sleep.

"I can't sleep. Not yet," Dieter said, his breath curling over the collar of his jacket. Ice began to bead on the zip, and above his own lip, clinging to the hairs on his cheek bones, and making his eyelashes tacky. He blinked and walked on.

The wind had blown the snow into shallow eskers, like an old three-dimensional map fashioned from layers and plates of cardboard. The going was straight, firm, and smooth, but not without danger. Dieter mustered the strength to walk over the black ice, reminding himself that it was thick enough to drive a car on, forcing himself not to look, not to second guess. He hoped the narrow lead ahead had not widened, and was relieved to find it had shifted, the two edges of the ice had moved closer. Dieter leaped over the gap and walked on.

At one point he thought of polar bears, only to forget all about them when he spotted the lights and activity around the *Ophelia* still a kilometre, maybe more, from where he stopped and stared. It was as if the carnival had arrived, disgorging the carnies, performers, and animals onto the ice, into tents pitched alongside boats instead of trucks, dogs instead of lions. Someone had turned on the *Ophelia*'s lights, and her mast was lit like a sparse Christmas tree, a single red and green navigation lamp, lost in the black polar night.

There were noises too, and Dieter realised that only the hungriest of bears would approach the whale carnival, with its Arctic revellers – howling dogs and high-spirited men. Even the heavens crackled, with the occasional shooting star arcing across the night sky beneath a curtain of green and white.

The carnival lights were celestial, the shadows of tent, boat, dog, and man, thin and angular with only the occasional beam of a snowmobile or even a car capable of catching Dieter in its glare as he approached. He noticed that the Greenlanders were laser focussed on the ice-bobbing sea. Only the dogs looked towards the mountains, relegated as they were to dormant modes of transport, as the men whooped, pointed, jabbered into mobile phones, and hurried to slide the flotilla of fibreglass skiffs and dinghies from the ice into the sea. Harpoons were raised, rifles loaded and slung, outboard motors dipped, and boats boarded. In the space of just ten minutes, Dieter and the dogs were alone on the ice, as the hunters chased thin spumes of mist far out to sea.

If he had binoculars, and if he knew where to look, if a Greenlander had stood by his side, placed a hand on his shoulder, and turned Dieter in the right direction, he might have seen pearl tusks and grey rubber flanks between the growlers of ice in the black sea. He might have seen the narwhal. But Dieter's eyes were drawn to another jewel, another prize, and he slipped between the tents, stepped over the anchor lines, and climbed the ladder onto the deck of the *Ophelia*.

Dieter opened the door to the cockpit and climbed down the short flight of steps. He flicked a switch and the cockpit lights blazed through the glass, bright squares lined with thick icy frames. The blood-soaked floor of the galley gave Dieter a start, and he steadied himself with a hand on the panel to his right.

It was clear where the victims had died, and *how* they had died – it was bloody. He shrugged and let the survivor in him guide him past the blood and deeper inside the yacht. He opened the door to the cabin on the right, found his duffel bag in the middle of the floor, as if it had fallen from his bunk. He unzipped it, slipped his hand around and between the clothes he had folded inside, and pressed his fingers into the space where he had hidden his thumb drive.

Dieter frowned, sat on his heels, and drew the duffel onto his thighs. He plunged his hand inside the bag again, and a third time. Then he switched on the light, emptied his clothes onto the deck, and ripped the bottom layer out of the bag. When everything was spread before him, and he had patted and unfolded every piece of clothing, checked inside every sock, Dieter threw the duffel bag against the sail bag in the pointed bow end of the cabin, tore off his hat, and gripped his head in his hands.

The dogs mistook Dieter's roar for a howl and joined in.

Chapter 9

Maratse heard the telephone ring three times before he understood what it was. He blinked, rubbed his eyes, and rolled over in his bed just as he heard Therese pick up the phone and answer the call. She answered in German, and, when she continued, he decided the call must be for her. He rolled onto his side and tugged the pillow over his head. He didn't hear Therese when she called to him, nor did he hear her run up the stairs in her bare feet. It was her perfume that pricked at his consciousness and forced him onto his elbows to stare at her. When she came into focus, he looked away.

"There's a woman on the phone. She wants to speak to you," Therese said.

"Hm."

"I told her she could call back, but she said she would wait."

"Okay," Maratse said, and rubbed his eyes, blinking in the glare of the light from the landing.

"You've got balls, Maratse," Therese said. "I only spoke to her for two minutes, and, if I were you, I wouldn't let her wait longer than it takes you to run downstairs." Therese giggled as Maratse pulled back the covers and slid out of bed. He stumbled on his way to the stairs, but only when he reached the top step did he feel it was safe to open his eyes.

"I'm not naked, Constable," Therese called, as he climbed down the stairs.

"Might as well be," he said, his mouth dry with sleep.

Maratse bit through the standard morning pain in his legs, before his muscles warmed up. He reached for the phone and pressed the receiver to his ear.

"Maratse," he said, and pressed his free hand against the windowsill as his legs trembled.

"Your girlfriend told me you were sleeping," Petra said.

Maratse waited for her to laugh, but when no laugh came, he felt compelled to answer straight away.

"She arrived yesterday, when I was out."

"And who is she?"

"The boat owner's daughter, I think."

"You don't know?"

"They have different surnames." Maratse looked up as Therese walked into the living room. Even the skin on her flat stomach had freckles. He looked away, caught his breath, and focussed on the pain in his legs – a necessary distraction.

"So you accepted the job."

"Not yet."

"I don't understand, David. There's a German woman living in your house?"

"Staying in my house…"

"Fine, let's call it that."

"What do you want, Piitalaat?"

"What do I want?" Petra caught her breath, and Maratse pictured her biting her lip. "How about you call me Petra from now on?"

"Hey…"

"In fact, let's just say, as far as you're concerned, my name is *Sergeant* Jensen."

"Don't be like that, Piitalaat. I didn't invite her

here."

Therese carried two mugs of coffee into the living room and placed one on the windowsill. She leaned close to Maratse and whispered into the handset that his coffee was ready, and then giggled as she walked to the sofa. Maratse stared at her as she unzipped her sleeping bag and pulled it over her bare legs. He pulled his eyes away from the flesh-coloured sports bra pinching her breasts and pressed his forehead against the cool glass of the window.

"She's leaving soon," he said, and wondered if Therese could speak Danish. When Petra didn't answer Maratse tried a different tack. "Sisse told me to say 'hi'."

"I'm sure she did." Petra sighed. "Listen, let's talk later."

"We can talk now."

"No," she said, "we really can't." Petra ended the call, and Maratse put the phone down. When he turned around to look at Therese she was smiling.

"She's a handful," she said, in English. The sleeping bag slipped as she bent her leg and tucked her knee against her chest.

"Her name is Piitalaat."

"Greenlandic?"

"*Iiji.*"

"But you spoke Danish."

"Piitalaat doesn't speak Greenlandic."

"Funny, her German is pretty good."

Maratse tugged his t-shirt over the waistband of his underwear, picked up his mug, and slumped in the chair opposite Therese.

"You said your name was Kleinschmidt."

"That's right."

"Not Berndt?"

"It's not important." Therese curled long freckled fingers around the mug and rested it on her knee. She stared at Maratse until he coughed and looked away. "You're wondering why I'm really here, aren't you?"

"*Iiji.*"

"I was in Ilulissat when daddy got news of what happened on *Ophelia*. He put me on the first plane to Qaarsut to come and take care of her."

"*Ophelia*?"

"Yes."

"You sail?"

"I have my Yachtmaster Ocean certificate. What about you?"

"Small fishing boats."

"Daddy always said it's not the vessel it's the water. I respect anyone who sails in these waters."

Maratse relaxed as the topic shifted to more familiar territory. If it wasn't for Therese's long legs and minimal sleeping wear, he might have enjoyed the conversation.

"Tell me what you want," he said, and sipped his coffee.

"I need to get *Ophelia* into a safe harbour, and I need the ship's log."

"Doesn't the captain have that?"

"No," Therese said. "She was unconscious when they took her off the boat. That's all I know."

Maratse nodded. "I found her like that."

"I know." Therese placed her empty mug on the table between them. She wrapped the sleeping bag around her waist and Maratse decided he could relax just a little bit more. "I need you to take me to *Ophelia*. Today."

"We would need permission from the police."

"Daddy's working on that. He says they might be

willing to let me sail her back to Ilulissat."

"Not without an escort," Maratse said. He wrinkled his brow as Therese tilted her head and smiled.

"That will be one of your jobs."

"I haven't said yes."

"No? That's strange when you consider that your bank account has an extra five thousand euros in it." Maratse frowned, and Therese said, "Our branch in Berlin confirmed the transfer this morning, while you were sleeping, before your girlfriend called."

"I didn't agree to that."

"I wouldn't worry; we tend to jump over that part. It's much easier to get someone to do what you want when the money is already in place. You'll get another three thousand once you have completed the other tasks Daddy wants you to do."

Maratse sighed. "What other tasks?"

"I'll let you know," Therese stood up, let the sleeping bag fall to the floor and tucked her thumbs into the panty elastic around her waist. "I'm going to get changed now. I suggest you do the same. We're going to be gone all day, longer if we get permission to sail." Therese plucked the elastic from her waist and let it snap against her skin. "Well?"

Maratse put his mug on the table and stood up. He heard the smooth slip of Therese's underwear on her skin as he climbed the stairs to his room. Things were moving just a little too quickly, and of their own accord. A helpless feeling wormed its way into his mind, and he gripped the thin duvet in his fist. Police work often had an element of helplessness attached to it, but this feeling was different, it had an edge, Maratse recognised it for what it was, he felt used.

He let his thoughts simmer as he dressed, tugging

on Karl's hand-me-down thermals that Buuti had brought over the day the sun disappeared for the winter. When he was ready, and had enough layers for a day on the ice, he opened the wardrobe and pulled his police jacket off the hanger. He ran his fingers over the dark square of material and loose threads where the police shield had once been attached, and pulled it on, amazed once again at how good it made him feel to wear it. He felt almost whole, stronger, empowered, and ready to steer this private investigation into something more agreeable.

Therese was right about one thing, he realised, it was easier to say yes to something when the decision had already been made. He might be in Berndt's debt, but Therese was in his country, and Greenland had its own rules, its own climate, and its own culture. Strengthened by the weight of the jacket on his shoulders, the pain in Maratse's legs didn't bother him as climbed down the stairs. Therese packed a small backpack in the living room as he pulled on his overalls, and tied the arms around his waist. Maratse pulled on his boots and opened the door.

"Where are you going?" Therese asked.

"To get the keys."

"Keys?"

"For the snowmobile. My dogs are staying here."

Maratse shut the door as Therese started to speak. He was halfway down the steps when the police Toyota bumped over the ice foot and drove onto the beach. Danielsen waved him over as Simonsen got out from behind the wheel, leaned against the side of the car, and lit a cigarette. The engine rumbled as Maratse crunched through the snow and accepted a cigarette from Simonsen.

"A peace offering," he said, as Maratse leaned in

to the flame from the lighter cupped in Simonsen's hands. Simonsen tucked the lighter in his pocket. "There's a woman in your house, Constable. Who is she?"

"Berndt's daughter." Maratse blew a cloud of smoke over his shoulder as Therese stepped onto the deck. He nodded at her as she lit a cigarette of her own, curled the hood of her jacket over her fiery-red hair, and watched them.

"Berndt called us this morning. He wants permission to sail his yacht to a safe harbour."

"She said the same."

"Did she also say he wants you on the boat with her?"

"*Iiji.*"

Simonsen glanced at Danielsen. "You see, it's this kind of thing that makes it difficult for me to like you, Maratse."

"I haven't done anything wrong."

"No, you haven't, but you always seem to be in the thick of it." Simonsen turned his head at the sound of the radio crackling inside the car. Danielsen reached inside to answer it. "I haven't made a decision yet. I need to wait for the investigative team to finish up." He paused as Danielsen spoke rapidly in Greenlandic. "What is it?" Danielsen held up one finger and looked away. Simonsen looked at Maratse. "What is he saying?"

Maratse translated, "Something has happened on board the yacht."

"I sent two policemen and a detective out there early this morning."

"Someone's been hurt." Maratse flicked his cigarette onto the snow as Danielsen leaned inside the car, clicked the radio into place, and then leaned over the bonnet to speak to Simonsen.

"The detective has been stabbed."

"On board the yacht?"

"*Aap.*" Danielsen held up his hand, as Simonsen reached for the door handle. "There's more."

"Go on."

"The assailant took the police car. He's driven off, deeper into the fjord."

Simonsen opened the door and climbed in behind the wheel. "Get in," he said to Maratse. He shifted into first gear as Danielsen climbed into the passenger seat, and Maratse opened the door behind Simonsen. He was half inside the vehicle when the door opposite him opened and Therese climbed in.

"This is not a taxi," Simonsen said. "Get out."

"That's my boat, Chief," Therese said, and shut the door. "I'm coming with you."

"This is police business. You're a civilian."

"So is he," she said, nodding at Maratse.

Maratse closed his door, as Simonsen cursed and accelerated off the beach, slipping the Toyota into four wheel drive to negotiate the ice foot.

"Don't," Maratse said, as Therese reached for the seatbelt and began to stretch it across her chest. "We might need to get out quickly." She nodded and let it slip back against the seat.

Simonsen accelerated through the gears, steering wide of the icy coastline, and following the peninsula to drive around the open lead of black water. Maratse noted the softer patches of ice as Simonsen raced across the frozen surface of the sea towards the hunters' camp in the distance. The moon lit the ice with a searchlight-white beam as the police emergency lights flashed blue against the bergs, and the winter dark was charged with colour.

Therese punched Maratse on the arm, her teeth flashing, her eyes green and bright, as Danielsen chattered on the radio, and Simonsen concentrated on the road ahead. Maratse wondered if Therese would be smiling if she knew the road was just twenty centimetres thick, perhaps less. He decided she probably would, shook his head and laughed, her excitement was infectious.

Maratse stopped laughing when he heard Danielsen ask the policeman to repeat what he had just said.

"What is it?" Simonsen said, as he downshifted to slow the Toyota. Maratse could see the dogs stirring as they approached the yacht.

"It's the detective. He was first on board. That's when he was attacked."

"All right." Simonsen glanced at Danielsen. "There's more?"

"*Aap.*"

"Spit it out."

"The assailant took the detective's gun."

"He's armed?"

Danielsen nodded as Simonsen slowed to a stop beside the yacht.

Simonsen turned in his seat and nodded at Therese. "Out," he said. "No discussion. You said it was your boat, I want you to get on it and stay on it."

Therese opened the door, and stepped onto the ice. She looked at Maratse, and said, "What about him?"

"He's coming with me." Simonsen nodded at Maratse, and then held out his hand to Danielsen. "Give me your sidearm."

Danielsen hesitated, and glanced at Maratse.

"I know what you are going to say, Aqqa, but I

need you here." He looked up as one of the policemen from Ilulissat jogged over to the Toyota. "Get the ambulance out here, and keep an eye on the German girl. Quickly."

Danielsen tugged his pistol from his holster, leaned between the seats, and pressed it into Maratse's hand. "I want it back," he said, and opened the passenger door. He slapped his hand on the policeman's shoulder and told him to get into the car. Simonsen shifted into first and accelerated into a tight turn as Therese joined Danielsen on the ice.

"Which way?" Simonsen said, as the policeman closed the passenger door.

"Northeast, past that pointy berg."

"How long ago?"

"Forty minutes."

Simonsen gritted his teeth, and then nodded at Maratse in the back. "Introduce yourselves."

"Inuk Taorana," said the policeman. "From Ilulissat."

"We've met," Maratse said, "a few years ago."

"Really?"

"You came to Ittoqqortoormiit on board *Sisak II*."

"Yeah, I remember. Maratse?"

"*Iiji*."

"Okay, enough introductions," Simonsen said. He pointed at a dark stationary shape between two icebergs. "Get ready, because that's my patrol car."

Maratse sat on the edge of the seat and peered through the windscreen as Simonsen slowed the Toyota to a crawl. Clumps of ice frozen into the surface crunched beneath the Toyota's tyres. Simonsen stopped the vehicle and turned off the emergency lights.

"Inuk," he said, "I want you to go to the right.

Maratse?"

"*Iiji?*"

"Go left of the bergs. I'm going to drive straight up to the car."

Maratse opened the door and stepped onto the ice. He stepped away from the car, gripped the pistol in both hands, and nodded once at Inuk as Simonsen pulled away. The engine rumbled, but beyond that, all was still, dark, and cold, as the moon retreated behind a thick cloud and it started to snow.

Chapter 10

Petra woke early on Sunday morning. The winter sun had yet to rise, and the Northern Lights blazed in the pre-dawn sky. She made coffee and stood at the window of her new apartment in Qinngorput and looked out over the bay towards the centre of Nuuk. The building cranes stood proud of the cityscape, lit in such a way that the stars might have fallen like snow to rest on the long metal arms, illuminating and approving Nuuk's steady climb to fame and fortune, a modern jewel in the Danish Crown waiting to be prised free of its colonial masters.

A flash of blue light caught Petra's attention. She tracked the police car's emergency lights from the harbour until they were lost, hidden, gone, as the weekend night shift wrapped up, and the day shift slipped out of their houses leaving families, loved ones, friends and pets to sleep on. Petra finished her coffee, turned her back on the Nuuk nightscape, and slipped under the covers of her bed. She picked up her smartphone and considered calling Maratse, and then slapped the phone, screen down, on the duvet as she remembered the woman, the German floozy, currently embedded in Maratse's tiny house in Inussuk.

"Embedded." Petra said the word aloud, and then swore. "So long as she hasn't *bedded* Maratse, I might still forgive him." She blew a strand of hair from her mouth as she wondered why it was so important. What would it matter if he did sleep with her? The heavy curtains absorbed her words, and Petra, alone in the dark, slipped another half metre beneath her duvet.

After a while she rolled over, picked up her phone and checked her social media. She saw that one of her colleagues had shared a link to a *Sermitsiaq* article about the murders in Uummannaq. Petra clicked on it, read the name of the journalist: Kitu Qalia, and then slid her finger down the screen as she read. According to a quote from the Chief of Police in Uummannaq, none of the crew had been charged yet, nor was there sufficient evidence to pursue the case. The next paragraph made Petra sit up, as Simonsen was further quoted to say that one member of the crew was still unaccounted for, and that they were keen to find him, and talk to him.

"Greenland's first manhunt," Petra said, and smiled.

There had been plenty of chases in Greenland that she knew of, and many more that were too old to interest her, and they were all affected by the weather. She knew that Maratse had once chased a murderer into the mountains around Ittoqqortoormiit. A Danish writer had tagged along, and published an article in an American magazine. Few people in Greenland had read it, and Petra wondered how much of it had been true. Knowing Maratse as she did, it wouldn't surprise her if all of it was true, but he rarely spoke of it. She smiled at the thought of another manhunt on Maratse's doorstep, and couldn't resist imagining him pursuing the killer across the ice and into the mountains.

She slapped the phone down on the mattress, and sighed at the sound of her own voice, muffled as it was beneath the duvet. "Get it together, *Piitalaat*."

Petra gave up trying to sleep and threw the duvet

further down the bed. She dressed in her workout clothes, prepared a bag, and then pulled on her salopettes and jacket, bracing herself for a moment before leaving her apartment, climbing down the stairs, and stepping out into the snow, swirling and drifting between the apartment blocks overlooking the bay. She found the keys to the car she was looking after for her Danish friends on vacation, cleared the windscreen, and then drove to the gym. Petra parked alongside the other insomniacs, and punched her code into the door.

The musky smell of sweat pricked at her nostrils as she peeled off her outer clothes in the changing rooms before stepping into the gym. Petra didn't recognise the Dane lifting weights in the corner, but guessed he might be on a temporary contract, with access to the gym a perk of the job. She knew the other man running on the treadmill far too well.

Petra pressed her water bottle into the holder of the machine next to Gaba Alatak, stretched, and then stepped onto the treadmill to programme her preferred distance and speed. Gaba tugged the ear bud out of his left ear as Petra began to run.

"You're up early," he said. The gym lights reflected in the sheen of sweat blistering his bare torso.

"Couldn't sleep." Petra allowed herself a single glance at her ex-lover's pectoral muscles and then concentrated on finding her running rhythm.

"I was at a meeting on Friday," Gaba said. "Your name came up."

"What meeting?"

"It was very interesting." Gaba grinned as Petra did a double step to lengthen her stride.

"You ape," she said. "Are you going to tell me

about it or not?"

"Not if you keep insulting me."

Petra picked up her water bottle and squeezed a mouthful into Gaba's face.

"Speak," she said.

"I tell you what, Sergeant," Gaba said, as he wiped the water from his face, "if you stop calling me names, and play nice, I'll let you buy me brunch at Katuaq when we're done here."

"Brunch? It's still too early for breakfast."

"You don't know how far I'm running."

Gaba pulled the remote from the holder next to his water bottle and turned on the television mounted on the wall in front of them. He flicked to the Teletext channel. Even in the technological wake of modernisation, some things never changed. KNR's Teletext channel had, somehow, been overlooked, but not forgotten. The news cycled in Greenlandic and Danish with one or two slow moving pages for each story.

Petra read the Danish news as she ran. She was just about to give in and invite Gaba to brunch when breaking news of the Uummannaq manhunt flicked onto the screen. She glanced at Gaba as she read about a policeman being stabbed with a knife, the suspect now considered armed and dangerous. Petra had to give the Teletext reporters credit; with a very limited amount of available text they had set the scene for a drama that would grip the nation. Even in the areas where internet was either unavailable or unaffordable, nearly every household had access to a television and the Teletext channel. She imagined Maratse following the story as it developed, and then remembered that his was one of the few households without a television. She decided to call him as soon as the sun was up in Nuuk.

"Have you heard anything about this?" Petra asked Gaba.

"Nothing. This is news to me."

"Do you think they will send you in?"

"The SRU? Maybe. That's up to Simonsen."

Petra read the same news item each time it cycled through the channel until her own running programme neared a close and she slowed. Gaba continued running.

"How long?" she asked.

"Just another five kilometres," he said, "maybe eight."

"I'll wait, and buy you brunch."

Gaba grinned, and said, "I thought you might."

"You're still an ape." Petra turned off her running machine, grabbed her water bottle and let Gaba run in peace.

She was dressed in her salopettes, the straps and bib hanging loose at her sides, with her jacket over one arm when Gaba walked out of the changing rooms. He nodded at his car and said he would meet her there. Petra wiped more snow from the windscreen and then drove to the Katuaq Cultural Centre. Gaba parked his SUV next to her Volkswagen, and followed her inside. They found a table and hung their jackets over the backs of the chairs, but as Gaba picked up his plate for the buffet brunch, Petra outlined the rules.

"Rules? For brunch?"

"Yes," she said."

"Like what?"

"This is not a date."

"Sergeant…"

"I used to be Petra, remember?"

"Yes."

"Then, we can agree, this is not a date."

"We agree."

"Second," she said, and pinched her middle finger.

"Are you giving me the finger?"

"I will, if you don't agree to rule two."

"All right. What is it?"

"You'll tell me everything."

"Everything I *can* tell you, yes."

"Fine," she said, and waved at the buffet tables, "you can eat."

Petra watched as Gaba weaved his way between the tables. She had to admit that the leader of Greenland's Special Response Unit took care of his body. She pushed the memories of that same body aside, pulled her smartphone from her pocket and called Maratse. She pressed the phone to her ear and waited for him to pick up.

"Piitalaat," he said, his voice a whisper with static from the wind making it hard to hear what he said.

"I can hardly hear you."

"I can't talk. Not now."

"Are you all right?"

"I'll call you," Maratse said, and ended the call.

Gaba put a plate of pancakes, sausage, and egg between his cutlery and picked up one of two empty coffee mugs. "Everything all right?" he asked.

"I just called David."

"Maratse?"

"Yes." Petra looked up. "I think he was on the ice. He said he couldn't talk." She frowned and said, "You don't think he's involved in the manhunt, do you?"

"I think our friend, the *Constable*, is always involved. One way or the other." Gaba tapped the table. "Don't worry about him. Get something to eat."

He waited as she bit at her lip. "Petra?" he said. "Breakfast?"

"Okay," she said.

Petra slipped her phone into her pocket, picked up her plate, and walked to the buffet. Gaba filled both mugs of coffee while she filled her plate. She smiled as she returned to the table – he had even remembered the juice.

"So," she said, as she pushed the thought of Maratse out of her mind, "what was this meeting about?"

"The one where they talked about you?"

"Yes," she said, and slapped the back of Gaba's hand with her fork.

"Sergeant?"

"I'll behave as soon as you stop teasing me."

"Deal," he said. Gaba took a sip of coffee, followed by a forkful of pancake. He grinned when Petra started tapping the table with the bottom of her knife. "Sergeant Jensen, you have been placed on a very short list of suitable applicants for a new policing initiative."

Petra made a face. "I don't want to babysit any more politicians, or visiting VIPs, show them around Nuuk, or…" She stopped when Gaba leaned back in his seat. She studied his face. "It's not that, is it?"

"*Naamik*."

"What is it then?" Petra put her knife down. She reached for her coffee, but barely tickled the handle with her fingers before Gaba started to speak, and she forgot about breakfast.

"It's like an Arctic task force, in fact, they might even call it that: *ATF*. Although," he said, and frowned, "I'm sure the Americans have something called that already."

"They have a lot of things." Petra smoothed a pile of crumbs from the tablecloth onto the floor. "Tell me."

Gaba leaned forwards. "Multidisciplinary, with officers from each and every Arctic nation. Yes," he said, as Petra opened her mouth, "even Russia."

"And they want me?"

"Your name is on the list."

"How long is the list?"

"Ah, Sergeant, that would be telling."

Petra thumped her glass on the table, spilling juice, and rattling the cutlery. She turned and apologized to the people eating at the tables nearby. "Are you on the list?"

"I'm not," Gaba said. "You look surprised?"

"Maybe I am," Petra said. She shook her head. "They'll want a Dane. Greenland is still Danish."

"No," Gaba said, "they want you."

Petra brushed long strands of her hair behind her ears and then cut a generous square of pancake. Her hair slipped loose again as she turned the pancake around the plate, idly chasing the maple syrup as her cheeks dimpled in a smile.

"You're a talented officer, Petra," Gaba said. "You speak three languages. You're single, no ties, and…"

"And?" Petra said.

"You're pretty good in bed too." Gaba ducked as Petra lifted the pancake on her fork. "Lower your weapon, Sergeant," he said. "I was joking, I didn't tell them that."

"But you told them the other things?"

"Yes," he said, and pushed back his chair. "And, if you're wondering, the commissioner told me to tell you. He thought I might see you over the weekend."

Gaba picked up his mug. "I'm getting a refill."

As Gaba moved away from the table to join the line of people waiting for fresh coffee, a Dane showed an American to the table beside Petra.

Petra took small bites of her breakfast as she thought about what Gaba had said. The thought might have lingered had it not been for the conversation between the two new arrivals. While Petra sipped at her juice she heard the American mention mining in Uummannaq fjord.

"What's the current status of the operation?" the Dane asked.

"Precarious," the American said, "and damned difficult to trace. There's a rumour of mining rights for the Svartenhuk area – legal documents, mind you, signed and stamped with official approval from the Danish and Greenlandic governments."

"And where are these documents? Who has them?"

"Arbroath Mining Co."

"They took over the mine in Marmoralik, Uummannaq?"

"Because of the extended rights," the American said, "I'm sure of it. Of course, these murders will slow things down."

Petra risked a glance and a smile when the American caught her eye. He said hello in English, and Petra answered with the little Greenlandic she knew. The American nodded and continued with his conversation. Petra turned back to her food, but continued to listen.

"So what has this got to do with the murders on some rich German's yacht?" the Dane asked.

"That depends on the purpose of his expedition. Berndt gave a statement to *Die Welt* when the story broke. He said the expedition had an environmental focus – something about microplastics…"

"Just following the current trend, eh?"

"Exactly, but he did let slip that his expedition team were also interested in exploring Svartenhuk to find the cabin built by Alfred Wegener."

"They want to find the cabin?"

"Perhaps," the American said, and lowered his voice. Petra stopped chewing. "But maybe they are looking for something else."

"Like what?"

"A journal, perhaps."

"Wegener's journal?"

"Yes." The American reached for his plate, and pushed back his chair. "You know what's in the journal?" He gave the table a theatrical rap with his knuckle. "Only Wegener's expedition notes, including a detailed geological survey and analysis of the Svartenhuk mountain range."

"Thorium?" the Dane whispered. "That's incredible."

"Who knows?" The American stood up. "Arbroath Mining is a very small company, just waiting for someone to buy them out."

"But if Svartenhuk has Thorium…"

"Yep," the American said. "Wegener's journal is quite the item of interest all of a sudden."

"I'll say," the Dane said. He stood up and walked with the American to the buffet table as Gaba sat down with a fresh mug of coffee.

"You've barely touched your food," he said. "Too excited to eat?"

"Something like that," Petra said. She turned and looked at the American as he took a selection of food from the buffet. The metal lid of the pan with scrambled eggs clanged as he put it down. "Do you know who that is?" Petra asked. "The American?"

"No," said Gaba, "but the Dane next to him works for GEUS. You know? The Geological Survey of Denmark and Greenland."

"Yes, I know what GEUS is."

"Anyway, he's new. Arrived last month. Why?"

"I don't know, but maybe I just found the motive for murder in Uummannaq."

Chapter 11

The winter was unseasonable. The thought pricked at Dieter's mind with every metre he drove on the sea ice in the stolen police patrol vehicle. It was the thought of driving on ice, not the act, which made him slow to a stop. He lowered his hands from the wheel and stared at the knife protruding from his stomach. Somehow, in the scuffle below decks, when the policeman had surprised him, Dieter had fallen, and the knife that had been in his hand was now in his stomach. His blood soaked through his thermal layers of clothing and into his waxed jacket, the cotton kind that needed to be waxed to be waterproof. The jacket was old, uncared for and now, without its protective wax, it was dark, saturated with his own blood.

He turned off the engine, and pushed his head back until he could feel the headrest pressing through his fleece hat. Dieter stared through the windscreen as snow swirled within the beam of the Toyota's headlights. He switched off the lights, and closed his eyes. He could still see the snow, floating in his vision, white flecks on a dark background, black like the sea, the death water beneath the ice.

The policeman had told him to stop, several times. Stop, Dieter mused, is the same word in a lot of the Anglo Saxon languages, but rarely had he heard it spoken in so many different ways as he did inside the yacht. The policeman commanded him to stop, ordered him, pleaded with him, and then begged him when Dieter's knife was pressing against the man's windpipe. But when Dieter had slipped, and the knife had burst through the lining of his own stomach, the policeman's tone had changed, softened, he had told him to stop as if there really wasn't an alternative, suggesting that if he didn't stop fighting and resisting, the knife in his stomach would cause more damage, it would not stop, and neither would the flow of blood.

It didn't.

Dieter didn't know if it was going to stop.

He gritted his teeth and fumbled the battery and the satellite phone out of the different pockets in his jacket as the air inside the Toyota cooled. Each time he moved the knife snagged on his jacket. Dieter fought back the nausea and grimaced through the pain as he assembled the satellite phone, turned it on, pointed the aerial towards the window, and dialled Marlene's number. His breath escaped his lungs in ragged bursts of frost, the choke of an ice dragon. Marlene answered on the third ring and Dieter's breath settled on the screen, as tears crackled into desiccated orbs in the corners of his eyes.

"Hi," he said.

"Dieter."

"Yes."

"You sound so far away."

"I am."

"I know, but more than that."

"I think I'm dying, Marlene."

"No," she said. "Don't you say that. It's not fair. That's not fair, Dieter."

"It's so peaceful here." Dieter turned his head. He looked at the iceberg on his left, brushed the knuckles of his left hand against the glass. He sighed as his breath froze upon the glass in a fractured steam of crystals, each breath adding another layer to the first. The steam obscured his view and he felt the stretch of cold skin as he wrinkled his brow and concentrated. Someone was saying something to him. "Marlene," he said.

"I need you to come home, Dieter. I need you home with me."

"So far."

"No, Dieter. It's not. You have to move. You have to stay warm."

Dieter dipped his chin and stared through his breath at the knife in his stomach. "Can't," he said.

"You can. Dieter," Marlene shouted. "You have to live."

Dieter felt something slide down his ear. Smooth, cold at the edges. His hand dropped to his side, and the satellite phone slipped between the handbrake and the seat.

"Marlene." Dieter tried to lift his hand. It slid off his lap and he let it dangle beside the seat cushion. He moved the tips of his fingers, tried to grasp the phone's stubby aerial. He wondered at the blue hue of the Northern Lights. "It's usually green," he said. "Flowing. Doesn't flash."

He didn't hear the command to get out of the car, didn't react at the sudden flash of white light that pinned him to the seat. Dieter closed his eyes, touched the tip of the phone. His head lolled to one side when the door opened, and there were voices, voices he could barely hear. Not German.

"We'll have to pack it," said Inuk. "We're not pulling it out here."

"*Iiji*," Maratse said. He opened the boot of the Toyota and pulled out the first aid kit. Maratse tore the paper wrappings and passed the bandages to Inuk.

Simonsen opened the passenger door, shining the powerful beam of his torch around the interior of the Toyota as Inuk and Maratse dressed Dieter's wound.

"There's no gun," said Simonsen. "What about his pockets?"

"Nothing," said Inuk.

"Wait." Simonsen reached over the handbrake and slipped his hand under the driver's seat. He pulled out the satellite phone, pressed it to his ear, and then placed it on the dashboard. "Dead battery," he said.

"We need to move him now," Inuk said.

"I'll bring the car."

The beam of Simonsen's torch lit the ice as he jogged to the police car. He backed up, stopped, and opened the boot. Simonsen fiddled with the cross-hatched guard and the backseat. When he had lowered it, Maratse and Inuk lifted Dieter out of one police car and into the other. Dieter groaned as they slid him across the carpeted interior. Maratse climbed in after him, cupped his hands under Dieter's knees, bending them as Inuk closed the door.

"I'll let the hospital know you are coming," Simonsen said, leaning through the driver's door. Then he stepped back to allow Inuk to climb behind the wheel. "I'll go back to the yacht." He slapped Inuk on the arm. "Keep me updated."

Inuk nodded, waited until Simonsen closed the door, and then shifted into first. Maratse searched for a comfortable position as Inuk accelerated across the ice towards Uummannaq.

"You sure he hasn't got a gun somewhere?"

Maratse checked Dieter's body, and said, "*Eeqqi.* No gun."

"Okay," Inuk said. "It's been a while since I drove on the ice so…"

Maratse was about to say something, but the sudden tilt of the front end of the Toyota thrust his body against the back of the driver's seat. The Toyota bobbed once, and then started to sink. Black water pooled at Inuk's feet, ballooning under the mat beneath the pedals.

"Shit," Inuk said. "Shit, shit, shit…"

"Inuk," Maratse said, as he worked back towards the rear door. "This way. Crawl over the seat." Maratse grabbed Inuk's arm and tugged him as the young policeman crawled between the seats. Black water swelled over the leading edge of the bonnet.

"Open the door," Inuk said.

Maratse fumbled with the handle. It moved like a hinge with no spring. The door did not open.

"It's child-locked."

The headlights of the second police car lit the boot with a triangle of white light, cut with Simonsen's black shadow as he raced to the back door of the Toyota and yanked it open.

"Out," he yelled, coughing in the Toyota's exhaust fumes as he gripped Maratse by the shoulder. Once Maratse was on the ice, Simonsen reached in and grabbed Inuk as he clambered over the bumper. The three of them dragged Dieter out of the boot and onto the ice as the Toyota dipped and the engine started to stutter. They ignored Dieter's groans and dragged him into the light of the headlights. The Toyota righted itself as the back wheels broke through the ice and the front end lifted. It bobbed in a square of black water. They watched as the sea rushed in through the open door at the rear and the fumes were stifled as the Toyota sank.

"Shit," Inuk said.

Maratse pointed at the ice, and said, "I'll walk in

front. Check it's safe."

Simonsen nodded. "Let's get him on the back seat."

Inuk opened the rear passenger door, and then helped the others lift Dieter onto the back seat. They laid him flat and shut the door.

"I'll drive," Simonsen said. He waited until Inuk was in the passenger seat, lit a cigarette and gave it to Maratse. "For the nerves," he said, and grinned.

Maratse raised his eyebrows, stuck the cigarette in the gap between his teeth, and picked a route around the thin ice. Simonsen climbed behind the steering wheel and shifted into first gear. He turned off the lights when Maratse turned and made a cutting movement with his hand across his throat.

Simonsen rolled down the window, and shouted, "Better with the emergency lights?"

"*Eeqqi*," Maratse said. "I can see better now." He walked on, the cigarette clamped in his mouth as he guided Simonsen to the left and right with his hands.

The *Ophelia*'s navigation lights were visible in the distance when Maratse waved Simonsen to a stop and walked to the passenger side of the vehicle.

"We've reached the older ice. We should be fine all the way back to the yacht."

"All right," Simonsen said. "Get in. I'll call Danielsen."

Inuk started to apologise as soon as Maratse closed the passenger door.

"No apologies needed," Simonsen said, once Danielsen was briefed. "It's paperwork and time, that's all. It could have been me who drove through the ice." He shifted into third gear. "This is my jurisdiction. I'm responsible. I'm just pleased we're all alive." He glanced in the rear-view mirror and caught Maratse's eye. "Even you, *Constable*."

Maratse nodded.

"There is just one thing," Simonsen said, as they approached the yacht.

"What's that?" Inuk asked.

"You owe me a car."

Simonsen stopped a short while later, as Danielsen climbed down the ladder onto the ice and jogged across to the car. "Everyone okay?" he asked.

"We're okay," Simonsen said. "A bit shook up."

Danielsen nodded at Inuk. "The ambulance will be here in a few minutes," he said, and pointed at a pair of headlights jerking across the ice towards them.

Maratse reached around Simonsen and handed Danielsen his pistol. "Thanks for the loan."

Danielsen nodded, and holstered the pistol. He pointed at the yacht. "The detective is okay. We found his gun in the cabin. It had slipped under the bed."

"And we found the knife," Simonsen said with a glance at Dieter on the back seat.

"What about Therese?" Maratse asked.

"She's been a little weird, emptying drawers onto the floor, going through all the lockers and crew kit bags. I had to stop her three times. I told her she was polluting the crime scene. She told me it was her boat. We went back and forth like that for a bit, and then I locked her in the bathroom." Maratse laughed as Simonsen ordered Danielsen to let her out. "You really want me to let her out?"

"Yes," Simonsen said. He took a long breath, and looked over his shoulder. "Stop laughing, *Constable*."

"*Iiji*," Maratse said, and opened the door. The ambulance pulled up alongside the police car. Inuk and Maratse helped the hospital orderly and nurse carry Dieter to the back of the ambulance, securing the stretcher between the wheel arches. Just before he turned away from the patient Maratse noticed something square pushing out of one of the cargo pockets of Dieter's trousers. He unzipped the pocket and pulled out a small leather-bound diary. It was fastened with a thin sealskin cord. Maratse slipped it into his pocket as he crawled out of the ambulance.

"I could go with him," he said, as he walked across the ice to Simonsen.

"Inuk will go with him," Simonsen said. "He needs to be in police custody. We have plenty of questions for him, as soon as he is able to answer them. Besides," he said, and smiled, "I need you to deal with the crazy German girl."

"On the yacht?"

"I'll send Danielsen back to get you, once we get everyone back to Uummannaq."

"That's okay," Maratse said. He looked at the teams of dogs tethered to the ice. "I'll borrow Karl's dogs."

"You're sure?" Simonsen said.

"Karl won't need them for another day. They'll butcher the whales they catch here, on the ice. I'll take Therese back to Inussuk, bring the dogs back tomorrow."

They turned their heads at a shout from the yacht. Maratse grinned as Danielsen took a step back from Therese as she climbed from the deck onto the ice.

"Maratse," she shouted, as she approached the police car. "We need to go."

"*Iiji*," he said, and gestured at the closest team of dogs. He waved at Danielsen as the young police constable got into the passenger seat. Inuk's colleague from Ilulissat helped the detective into the rear of the police car, and, a few moments later, Simonsen pulled away, following the ambulance along the trusted ice route to Uummannaq.

"There goes our ride," Therese said. She slapped her hands against her thighs, and said, "Wonderful. Now how do we get back?"

Maratse coiled a dog whip into his hand, and said, "You're sure you don't want to stay on the yacht?"

"It's not there."

"What isn't?"

"The digital log. Katharina Fischer, the captain, made a backup of the ship's log each night, and saved it to a thumb drive. They couldn't always establish a link with the satellite, so she didn't send the last few updates. Her laptop is missing too." Therese jabbed a finger at the rear lights of the vehicles. "I should have gone with them. I bet one of the crew has it."

"The laptop?"

"Yes, or the thumb drive. I really need to talk to them."

"What would the log tell you?"

"The basics, coordinates, position. That kind of thing." Therese took a step closer to Maratse. She tilted her head, and said, "What happened out there? Why did you only come back in one vehicle? What about the man, Dieter?"

"Is that his name?"

"Yes."

Maratse pulled Karl's sledge off the wooden box and onto the ice. He explained what had happened, and pointed at the vehicles disappearing into the polar night. "There was no room for us. I said we would go home by dog sledge."

"Great," she said. "The slow way home."

"Are you in a hurry?"

"Yes, actually."

Maratse turned his back on her and Therese snorted. She pointed at the dogs.

"Fine, which ones do we take?"

"You can handle dogs?"

"Sure." She took a step towards the team. "Which ones?"

"That one." Maratse pointed at a large, black male, with two cream spots of fur above its eyes. "And those three." He watched as Therese marched towards the dogs, clamped them one at a time between her knees, unclipped them, and brought them to Maratse.

Ten dogs later, and Maratse nodded that he had enough. Therese sat at the rear of the sledge, and Maratse gave the order for the dogs to run. The sledge creaked across the ice, bumped over the ridged tyre tracks, and settled onto the smoother, thinner ice close to the shore. Instead of sledging around the open leads of water, Maratse used the whip to guide the team to the narrowest part, encouraging the dogs over the crack in the ice with clicks of his tongue and short, repetitive commands. He let the whip trail behind the sledge after the lead, and tucked the handle beneath a length of cord. The edge of the journal dug into Maratse's thigh as he stretched his legs.

"Tell me about Dieter," Therese said. "Do you think he is the killer?"

"Maybe?" Maratse said. "I don't know. But now all the crew are accounted for, maybe you can sail the boat back to Germany?"

"I still need that log."

Maratse reached for the cigarettes in his pocket, and then let his hand slip to his lap. The journal in his pocket weighed heavier on his mind than the need for a cigarette. The thought occurred to him that he was withholding evidence, but something suggested it was the right thing to do. He thought about that as the dogs increased speed, encouraged by the scent of home.

Chapter 12

Petra parked outside the police station, shrugged her backpack over her shoulders and locked the car. The snow crunched beneath her boots as she walked across the car park. She stopped to wave as the police Commissioner Lars Andersen pulled up alongside her. He wound down his window and beckoned for her to come over.

"Good morning, sir," she said.

"Sergeant," he said, and nodded at the passenger seat. "Get in."

Petra walked around the front of the car, kicked the snow from her boots and then opened the door. "Where are we going?" she asked as she sat down on the passenger seat.

"I have decided to buy you breakfast." The Commissioner reversed into an empty spot and pulled out of the car park. He stopped to make a quick phone call to his assistant. "Have someone clear Sergeant Jensen's schedule too," he said, and ended the call.

"You officially have my interest now, sir." Petra buckled her seatbelt and dumped her backpack in the foot well.

"You mean I don't always?" The commissioner attempted a glare, before his face relaxed and he laughed. "Relax, Sergeant, that was a joke."

"I knew that," Petra said. They stopped at a T junction and Petra waved to a group of young Greenlanders crossing the road.

"Actually," the commissioner said, "I talked to Simonsen in Uummannaq early this morning. One of their cars went through the ice last night."

"What? I didn't hear about that. Was anyone hurt?"

"Everyone is fine. One young constable from Ilulissat is a bit shook up, but everyone got out in time." The commissioner put the car in gear and pulled out into a space in the stream of early-morning traffic. "Maratse was in the car."

"What?"

"It's okay, Petra, he is fine."

"What was he doing in the car?"

"It seems that Simonsen deputised him, if you can believe that." The commissioner chuckled. "It must be my fault. I was the first to bring Maratse out of retirement. Remind me never to do that again."

"That was an extreme situation, sir."

"So was this, apparently. Maratse got caught up in the search for the missing crew member."

"I did read about that."

"Dieter Müller is his name. He is now in custody. To be more precise, he is in hospital with a constable outside the door."

"They caught him?"

"He had a knife in his belly." The commissioner drove to the harbour and along the quay. He parked beside the steps leading to the deck of a United States Coast Guard Legend-class cutter. Petra read the name stencilled on the bow: *Logan*. The commissioner pointed at the bow of the ship. "This is where we are having breakfast, but, before we go on board, I need us both to be clear, once again, that we don't talk about Maratse."

"Sir?"

"There's a lot of fallout still surrounding the activities of the ex-Sirius Konstabel Fenna Brongaard. She seems to have a hard time doing anything quietly. You'll find that the Americans are just as interested in her as the Canadians, the Chinese..." He sighed. "Everybody, really. I think they would all like an intimate chat with our favourite, and retired, Constable Maratse, and I'm doing everything I can to keep his whereabouts and availability as vague and unconfirmed as possible."

"Thank you, sir."

"Of course, if he could just stay out of trouble, for a year or more, it would make things a lot easier. You understand?"

"More than you know," Petra said.

"Right, now about this meeting."

"Yes?"

"Did Gaba talk to you?"

"He did."

"Good. He might not always show it, but he thinks very highly of you, Petra, as do I."

"Thank you, sir."

"Don't thank me before you know what you are getting into. Now, before we go on board, I want you to be aware of something." Petra waited as the commissioner checked a text message on his mobile. He tapped a quick reply and slipped the phone back into his pocket. "They're ready for us."

"You were saying something, sir. Before the text."

"Right, there is an American on board, a civilian, and I honestly don't know what his role is, or why he is here, but I want you to be on your guard, and not just because of Maratse."

"Sir, Gaba said I was being recommended for a

joint task force covering the Arctic. He talked about police, not spies."

"When it comes down to issues of sovereignty and borders," the commissioner said, "the differences between the two tend to get a little blurred. I have a feeling this particular American is interested in the *Ophelia*."

"The yacht in Uummannaq?"

"Exactly. Which is why I'm putting you on the case. You're going to liaise with Simonsen, but you will report directly to me. Understood?"

"Yes, sir." Petra slipped her hand around the door handle. "It's an American ship, sir, how will I know which American is the one to be wary of."

"I have confidence in you," the commissioner said, "but as a general rule of thumb, I would suggest being wary of them all."

"All Americans?"

"It couldn't hurt." The commissioner laughed, as he opened the door. "I was joking, Sergeant."

"That's two bad jokes in one day, sir."

"I'm doing well, aren't I?"

Petra got out and closed her door. She followed the commissioner up the steps leading to the deck of the *Logan*. They handed in their sidearms to a security detail waiting for them at the top of the stairs, signed a form, and took turns to be searched before being escorted inside the ship. Petra worked hard to dampen her excitement, to control it, but the smile she wore was as stubborn as Maratse. She thought about him as she followed the coast guard officer to the wardroom below decks. She couldn't quite imagine how Maratse had become involved in the manhunt, and she was having difficulty believing that it was Simonsen who suggested it. Petra decided Simonsen must have been under a lot of pressure, but stopped thinking about it when the officer in front of her stopped outside a door and knocked. She took a breath, smoothed the front of her jacket, and straightened her back.

"See," the commissioner whispered with a nod at their escort, "you're already infected."

"What?" Petra frowned, and then studied the ramrod position of attention the officer held before the door was opened and they were invited inside.

The wardroom was cramped but well-equipped. One of the bulkheads doubled as a flat screen, displaying the desktop of a Windows computer. There were two printers and a shelf of laptops fixed at the opposite end of the room, together with a coffee machine, and what looked like an old photocopier and a fax.

"Sergeant Jensen?" said the man who opened the door. He shook her hand, and said, "My name is Inspector Etienne Gagnon. I'm with the Royal Canadian Mounted Police." He gestured at the table filling the room and introduced, "Evelyn Odell with the Alaska State Troopers, Vitaly Kuznetsov from the Russian Militsiya." Petra waved hello, as Gagnon continued by pointing at a tall man in a wool sweater standing to one side of the screen. "This is Hákon Sigurdsson from the Icelandic State Police. The task force is still in the early stages of development. We're waiting on confirmation of the representatives from Finland, Norway, Sweden, and Denmark."

"Denmark?" Petra asked.

The commissioner coughed as he sat down. "We're lucky enough to have two representatives on the task force." He unzipped his jacket and accepted the offer of a coffee from the Icelander. Petra sat down beside him.

"The *Logan*," Gagnon said, as Sigurdsson placed a tray of mugs on the table, "will function as the mobile base of operations. The idea is that each country will take turns providing the task force with a ship, and a helicopter. The US has the first watch."

"Okay," Petra said. She sipped her coffee and tried not to stare too hard at the different members of the team. This wasn't how she had imagined her Monday was going to start.

Sigurdsson walked around the table and pulled out the chair opposite Petra. She noted that all of the team members were in good physical shape, all under thirty. Odell shared the same long black hair and coffee-coloured skin as Petra, and she wondered if she was a Native Alaskan. She wondered too who would lead the task force.

"If you're wondering who the boss is," Gagnon said, with a smirk, "it's a bit of an inside joke."

"I don't understand," Petra said.

"He means you don't have one, yet," the commissioner said. "Nor do you have a name."

"Polarpol has my vote."

Petra turned just as a new face entered the room. He looked American, and, when he stopped to shake her hand, she realised she had seen him before.

"You speak English," the man said.

"Yes," Petra said.

The man let go of her hand, and said, "You must be a quick learner, as I don't recall you could yesterday."

Petra felt a sudden heat in her cheeks. She glanced at the commissioner, and then looked up at the man. "I apologise."

"Don't do that," he said. "But don't imagine you fooled me either." He placed his gnarled hands on the back of the chair beside Petra, and looked at each of the team members in the room. "How about you guys take a break? Take a ride into Nuuk, I can recommend the Katuaq café," he said, with a glance at Petra.

"We were just getting started," Gagnon said.

"I'm sure you were, Inspector. Now, take a break."

The man waited until the room had emptied but for Petra and the commissioner. The Icelander paused to say something in Danish to Petra, but the American ushered him out of the room with a firm hand on his arm. He closed and locked the door once the Icelander stepped into the corridor.

"Didn't Iceland used to be a Danish colony?" he said, as he poured himself a mug of coffee.

"They became independent shortly after World War Two," the commissioner said.

"So they can speak Danish?"

"Yes."

"As do the Greenlanders?"

"We do," Petra said.

"So this *Polarpol*," the man said, "could just as easily be called *DanPol*, seeing as the Swedes and the Norwegians speak a similar language." He took a sip of coffee, and then smiled. "I'm joking," he said.

"Save me," Petra whispered. The commissioner kicked her leg and she hid her smile behind her mug.

"Sergeant Jensen," the man said, "my name is Samuel Johnson. For the purpose of this briefing you will assume that I'm with the United States Geological Survey. You can call me Sam."

Petra said nothing.

"Furthermore, you will not repeat anything said inside this room to anybody, unless the commissioner or I tell you to do so. Do you understand?"

"Yes," she said.

"Good." Sam reached for the remote in the centre of the table and used it to control the mouse on the screen. He clicked to open a folder. "Do you have any questions about your briefing?"

"What briefing, sir?"

"I told you everything you needed to know over brunch, yesterday. Unless, you believe that was purely coincidental?"

Petra looked at the commissioner. He shrugged and turned his attention to the screen as Sam opened a PDF document with a photo of a man stapled to the top right corner.

"Let's assume you remember everything I said," Sam said. He pointed at the photo of the bearded man in the document. "Do you know who that is?"

Petra pointed at the text below the photo. "It says his name is Berndt, but I have never seen or heard of him before today."

"Berndt is a person of interest to us," Sam said, "as is his so-called daughter: Therese Kleinschmidt." Sam clicked on a second document. "She is currently in Uummannaq. It seems the Berndts have hired a local to help them. I believe you both know this man." Sam clicked a new document onto the screen. Petra bit her lower lip as she looked at a recent picture of Maratse. "Tell me, Sergeant Jensen, just how well do you know David Maratse?"

"I have worked with him."

"More than that?" Sam asked. "Any personal entanglements you think I should be aware of?"

"No," Petra said. "None."

"You said Maratse had been hired to help Berndt," the commissioner said. "With what, exactly?"

"As I told the sergeant yesterday, it is our belief that Berndt is looking for evidence to prove that the Svartenhuk area is rich in thorium. If it is correct, then that would make this particular range a very wealthy piece of real estate, especially for the company who owns the rights to mine in that area."

"Arbroath Mining," said Petra.

"I'm impressed, Sergeant, you *were* listening after all."

"What proof do they need?" she asked.

"This is the fun bit," Sam said. "Do you like treasure hunts?" He moved the cursor to a new folder and clicked another document onto the screen. "This is Alfred Wegener," he said, "a renowned polar researcher, who, as you probably know, died in Greenland, on the inland ice sheet, in November 1930. He was German, which, if you will allow me to digress," Sam clicked on a fifth document, "makes your secondment to the Arctic Task Force, quite interesting all of a sudden. Do you agree, Sergeant?"

Petra gripped her mug in both hands as she stared at a file with her photo, name, and a brief service record.

"It's all right, Sergeant. Denmark and the United States are allies, friends, if you will, and friends share information." He circled her name with the cursor, and said, "Piitalaat? Is that Greenlandic?"

"Yes," she said.

"But no-one calls you that, do they?"

Petra looked at Sam, caught the glint in his eyes, as he stared back at her.

"It's a lovely name, although I'm sure I didn't pronounce it properly. Anyway," Sam clicked back to the Wegener document. "Berndt believes that Wegener presented a misleading report of the mining potential for Svartenhuk. And we believe he wants to find the clue that will lead him to the treasure."

"And what is that?" the commissioner asked.

"Wegener's missing journal," Sam said.

"Forgive me," the commissioner frowned, as he tapped a finger on the table, "I did not have the benefit of Sergeant Jensen's briefing. Why would Wegener deliberately write a misleading report?"

"Who knows? Perhaps he fell in love with the area."

"And what will Berndt do with the journal?"

"Destroy it," Petra said.

"What?"

"Good girl," Sam said.

Petra pointed at the screen, and said, "If the journal is destroyed, no-one can prove the existence of minerals in that area without another expedition."

"So," the commissioner said, "the Danish Technology University can send a bunch of students up there next summer."

"They won't do that," Sam said. "Tell him why, Sergeant."

Petra understood that she was being tested. She folded her hands on the table in front of her, and said, "If Svartenhuk is as rich as Berndt believes it is, he will want to keep the information a secret so he can buy the mining company that has the rights, for very little money."

"But he can't stop the Danish or Greenlandic government from carrying out a survey next summer," the commissioner said.

"No," Petra said, "but he can use the media to make it very difficult for the government, any government, to commission the survey."

"How?"

"By appealing to the people of the world to think of the families of those murdered in Svartenhuk, and by making it very difficult for a survey team to explore the area without being labelled as insensitive. He would suggest they wait at least another year."

"By which time he will have convinced his board to buy the struggling company sitting on the Svartenhuk mining rights." Sam closed the open documents with a click of the remote, and turned the screen off. "Well done, Sergeant."

"Yes," the commissioner said, "very good, but answer me this, Sergeant, are you saying the murders were planned for that purpose?"

"I don't know, it just came to me, sir. But if you are asking me if people are prepared to kill for the secrets in Svartenhuk, I think they already have."

Chapter 13

Maratse clumped down the stairs, glancing at Therese asleep on the sofa, one long freckled leg curled over the sleeping bag, as he walked to the kitchen. He decided on fresh coffee, and held a jug beneath the tap. The water limped up the pipes and the electric pump juddered with little or no resistance.

"I told you, I emptied the tank," Therese called from the living room. She appeared at the kitchen door in her pants and bra, forcing Maratse to look away.

"I'll get more water," he said, and brushed past her.

Therese stopped him with her arm. Her skin seemed to glow and Maratse could feel the heat from her body through his t-shirt as she pressed in close to him. "What did you find when you searched Dieter?"

"Nothing."

"I'm not so sure," Therese said. She shifted position and brushed her hand across the wispy black hairs of Maratse's oriental beard. "I told you I liked this style, didn't I?"

"*Iiji.*"

"Then why don't we find out how much? What do you say?"

Maratse took Therese's hand and peeled it from his cheek. He looked into her green eyes, spared a glance at the blush of freckles across her cheeks, her nose, her lips, and said, "I didn't find anything."

Maratse let go of Therese's hand and walked into the living room.

"Where are you going?"

"To fill the tank with water." He pulled on his overalls, boots, and hat, and stepped outside.

Inussuk had a water tank with a pump in a small insulated wooden building behind the store. It was blue, just like all the utility buildings in Greenland. Hospitals were yellow, stores and schools painted a dark red, police houses were green. Maratse collected two twenty litre plastic jerry cans from beneath the deck of his house, and carried them to the water tank. His boots slid over the finger-thick rime of spillage ice on the metal grate beneath the tap. Maratse unscrewed the cap of the jerry can, lined up the mouth with the spigot, and pushed the button to pump the water; he repositioned the can, and waited for it to fill. Buuti surprised him with a pinch to his waist.

"You're up early," he said, as he switched cans, and capped the first one.

"Karl has caught a whale," she said. The light of the water station danced in her eyes, and she pressed a set of keys into Maratse's hand. "He wants you to bring the snow scooter."

"*Iiji.*"

"But not the woman," Buuti said. "He thinks she is a journalist."

"He's probably right," Maratse said, and tucked the keys into his pocket. "Her father owns a media company."

"I'm not ashamed," Buuti said.

"Of what?"

"Hunting whales. But they don't understand, do they?"

Maratse screwed the cap onto the second jerry can

and straightened his back.

"Europeans?"

"Non-Arctic people."

"I think there is a big distance between them and their meat." He shrugged, and said, "I'll fill the tank and then go and get Karl."

"*Qujanaq*," Buuti said. "We have narwhal for Christmas." Buuti smiled, wriggled her shoulders within her jacket and walked back to her house.

Maratse picked up the cans of water, grunted with the strain, and then carried them inside the house to fill the tank. Therese was in the bathroom, and he called out that he was leaving.

"I'll be back in a few hours," he said.

He waited for a reply, and, when none came, he pulled on a few extra layers and left the house. Maratse tugged a thick fleece neckie from his overalls, and slipped it over his head. He pulled on the gauntlets tucked beneath the seat of the snowmobile, checked the tank, and started the engine, grinning at the sudden roar of power. Maratse considered himself a traditional hunter. As long as there was ice, he would never give up his dogs. But the warning signs were clear, and, despite the welcome cold snap and the lack of wind that allowed the sea ice to cover the fjord, he knew it was far from the norm. The days of the sledge dog were disappearing, even north of Uummannaq. Perhaps in ten years, maybe fifteen, the number of dogs in Uummannaq would be reduced to a handful, kept for show, or for the dwindling stream of tourists failing to come further north than Ilulissat. Maratse didn't know exactly how he felt about that, he tried not to feel, to think; mostly he just wanted to live.

He let the engine idle for a moment, tugged one of

the gauntlets off his hand, pulled out his mobile, and dialled Petra's number.

"Piitalaat," he said, when she answered.

"You didn't call."

"When?"

"After the car went through the ice. Why didn't you call?"

"I didn't think."

"*I* would have called," she said, "but I heard it from the commissioner. He said Simonsen took you on the search, and that's why you were in the car."

"*Iiji.*"

"David," Petra said. Maratse heard her take a breath. "If we are going to be friends…"

"We *are* friends, Piitalaat."

"If we are going to be more than that, one day, I really need to know about things like this."

The snow crunched beneath his boots as he paced around the snowmobile. "I'm sorry," he said. "But I'm calling now."

"And I'm pleased. Pleased you are calling, and that you are all right. I'm sorry too," she said. "It's been quite a morning. I want to tell you about it."

"I'm here."

"I know, and I'll tell you, when I see you."

"I don't know when that will be," Maratse said. "I have to help Karl, and…"

"I know," Petra said. "I'm flying to Qaarsut today. I'll see you this afternoon." She paused, and said, "The commissioner wants me to interview the crew of the *Ophelia*. I'm liaising with him, and…"

"And?"

"Some other people. I'll tell you when I see you."

"This afternoon?"

"Yes."

"I'll pick you up."

"I'd like that."

Maratse ended the call, slipped the mobile into his pocket, and pulled on the gauntlet. He ignored the discomfort in his leg as he lifted it over the seat and made himself comfortable on the snowmobile. He clicked it into gear and throttled up and over the drift of snow before racing past the dogs, slowing to negotiate the ice foot, and then accelerating onto the sea ice. Karl looked after his snowmobile, and Maratse increased speed to a steady seventy kilometres an hour. On a straight stretch of smooth ice he pushed it over one hundred, the wind biting at his cheeks, the bubbles and bumps of ice rattling through the skids and vibrating into his body. Even traditionalists are allowed to have a little fun, he thought. Maratse patted one hand against his chest pocket, and then gave up the idea of smoking as the left skid jarred on a stubborn clump of ice, and Maratse was forced to steer with both hands, wrangling the metal beast onto an even course. He throttled down to eighty and concentrated on the ice ahead. The moon reflected on the new layer of snow that had covered the ice in patches through the night, and the deep blue of the polar sky pushed at the fringes of the black night and suggested that a new day was dawning, although the sun would not rise for another two months.

The smell of blood and intestines steamed in the distance, as Maratse approached the edge of the ice. A single floe, covered in blood, had broken free of the edge, with one hunter securing it with the tip of his ice staff while another worked on the carcass of a narwhal. Maratse had seen blood floes before, thick plates of ice where hunters had butchered a whale. In the winter they would steam until the heat had long since left the carcass, the hunters motoring home in bloody fibreglass skiffs with a bounty of food for the winter. Maratse understood Buuti's concern, and imagined the uproar the western media would have at the sight of so much blood, the sprawl of intestines with a heavy tang of hot cabbage, and the positioning of toothed heads cut flat to stand on the ice as the men worked. This was not an industry, it was a livelihood, meat for the family, the tooth sold whole or carved into earrings and *tupilaq* – small figures polished to a smooth creamy finish – so much richer and ornate than those carved in reindeer bone. Tourists were not allowed to buy products made of narwhal, but there were plenty of Danes looking for a souvenir. As long as they lived in Greenland for six months or longer, they were free to take such rich treasures home.

Maratse found Karl and Edvard wrapping huge steaks of dark red meat in plastic tarpaulins. The dogs jerked back and forth, to the very limits of their tethers, intoxicated by the smell. Karl grinned at Maratse as he cut the snowmobile's engine. He beckoned to him and pulled back a corner of the tarpaulin under which Maratse saw a stack of thick grey-mottled skin and blubber. Karl took the knife in his bloody hand and carved a finger-thin length of whale skin – *mattak* – and pressed it into Maratse's hands. Maratse reached deep into a pocket and pulled out a small knife, grinning as he clamped the *mattak* between his teeth and cut a chunk free. He wiped a smear of spit and fat from his lips and nodded at Karl.

"Good," he said, and grinned.

"Six whales," Karl said, and pointed at the men working on the ice. "And there is another pod on the way." He pointed at a man standing alone at the edge of the ice. "The game officer says we can take another three. That's nine for Uummannaq. Not enough," he said, with a shake of his head.

"Buuti is pleased," Maratse said.

"I know," Karl said. He wiped a bloody hand across his brow. "I must work, or I'll get cold." He nodded at the overalls, rolled down and tied around his waist by the sleeves.

"Here," Edvard said, as he stood up. He pressed the wooden handle of a thick blade into Maratse's hand. "I just sharpened it," he said, and tapped the blade with a bloody fingernail. It wasn't the first time it had been sharpened that night, nor was it the first time it had been used. The blade was narrower than the hilt of the handle, curving in a smooth arc to the point. Both sides of the blade were scratched from use, the grains of the handle filled with blood. Edvard pointed at the carcass he was working on and Maratse kneeled beside him and got to work.

The trick, he knew, was to cut a handle in the thick whale skin, and then carve a square around it, teasing, cutting, and pulling the skin from the meat until a square of skin and blubber was released roughly the size of a school atlas, thicker than a fist. Maratse stopped to shrug out of the top half of his overalls, tied the sleeves around his waist, and continued. Edvard smoked as he cut, and Karl's blade was not idle. They were finished with the whale an hour later.

"You go back," Edvard said to Karl. "I'll stay and help my brother-in-law."

"Okay," Karl said. He slapped Maratse on the back, and they wrapped the meat in another tarpaulin, securing it to the sledge with lengths of cord tied around the wooden thwarts and pulled in a zigzag across the bloody prize. Karl whistled, and said, "I can taste Buuti's narwhal stew already. And," he said, patting the stack of *mattak*, "she promised to fry the *mattak* and marinate it with onions, vinegar and…"

"And?"

"Something else. Something delicious."

"Aramat?" Maratse said, with a thought to the classic spice mix in every Greenlander's kitchen."

"*Naamik*," Karl said, with a wrinkled brow. He waved his hand. "That's for fin whale or *sildepiske*. This," he said, and patted the tarpaulin, "is narwhal."

Maratse laughed. He climbed onto the snowmobile and shunted it into position in front of the sledge with gentle twists of the throttle. Karl attached the sledge to a thick loop of rope at the back of the snowmobile, and climbed onto the seat behind Maratse. He clapped the retired policeman on the back, and Maratse shifted into gear, driving around the dog teams on the ice before opening up the throttle and racing towards Inussuk. Karl lit two cigarettes, and pushed one between Maratse's lips. The smoke drifted across their bloody brows, tickled the clogged pores of their blood-stained fingers, and blew across the bounty of meat and *mattak* on the sledge.

"I heard about the police car," Karl shouted in Maratse's ear.

"*Iiji*."

"You were inside it."

Maratse nodded.

"But you are all right?"

"I am."

"What about the man? He stabbed a policeman."

"Maybe," Maratse said. "Piitalaat is coming to interview him."

"She's coming today?"

"*Iiji.*"

"That's nice. She must come to dinner. Perhaps she has never tried narwhal?"

"Do you think there is enough?" Maratse chuckled a cloud of smoke from his lungs.

"There is never enough," Karl said. He leaned back in his seat, finished his cigarette, and flicked the butt onto the ice.

High tide had pushed the ice foot into a thick slippery wall that took some time to negotiate. Karl guided the sledge from the back, leaning into the uprights as Maratse tried to pull the sledge up and over the ice. After twenty minutes, and under the silent gaze of a small crowd, Karl unhitched the snowmobile and Maratse parked it on the sea ice. They fetched a team of dogs and pulled the sledge up and over the ice foot, all the way to Karl's house. A group of six small children, Nanna among them, raced after the sledge. The dogs whirled with the smell of fresh meat, and Karl found a bucket of entrails to reward them once Maratse had secured them at the ends of their chains. It was only when the meat was in Karl and Edvard's freezers that Maratse realised the lights were not on in his house, and Therese was nowhere to be seen.

"A taxi came from Qaarsut," Buuti said, as she handed Maratse a square slab of *mattak*.

"Qaarsut?"

"*Aap.*"

"Not Uummannaq?"

"*Naamik.* I think she is leaving."

"Leaving?"

Maratse pressed the *mattak* under his arm as he ran up the stairs and into his house. He left the whale skin on the mat and clumped upstairs, ignoring the bloody ice cascading from the soles of his boots. He threw back the sheets on his bed, and tossed the pillow onto the floor. The journal was gone.

The thunder of the four rotors of the de Havilland Dash 7 shook the house as it descended for a short landing on the icy strip in Qaarsut. Maratse raced down the stairs, out of the house, and along the beach to the snowmobile.

"What's the rush?" Karl yelled, but Maratse ignored him.

The engine started at the first turn of the key, and Maratse felt the snowmobile leap across the ice as he accelerated. He pushed the machine from seventy, past ninety, felt his arms start to shake as the snowmobile shuddered around one hundred and thirty kilometres an hour. Maratse squinted through the cold air pricking his cheeks into solid cubes of flesh. He saw the lead of open water, another one, about ten seconds after he should have decreased speed to turn to avoid it. Instead, committed, Maratse increased speed, gritted his teeth, and held his breath as the skids skimmed across the first metre of the open lead, crashing into and biting at the brittle edge half a metre further away. Maratse felt the rear of the snowmobile dip into the water, felt the splash of icy water as it sprayed across his overalls, and then felt nothing more than relief as the snowmobile found purchase on the other side of the lead, and the leading edge of the tracks spun and gripped the ice, propelling Maratse forwards, and out of the sea. Maratse slowed for a second to study the ice ahead, steered around the thicker patches of snow that would warm and degrade the ice below, choosing instead to race along a path of black ice. That route, more cracks, and a few open leads, took him deeper into the fjord, away from the runway. The first passengers would have disembarked by now, he realised, Petra among them. But it wasn't Petra he was racing to meet. Maratse knew that he had maybe twenty minutes before the Dash 7 took off again, together with Therese Kleinschmidt and Alfred Wegener's lost journal, the one worth killing for.

Chapter 14

The Dash 7 was still parked outside the airport building when Maratse bumped the snowmobile up and over the ice foot beside the dock in Qaarsut. He swerved to avoid a string of loose sledge dog puppies and then powered up the road. When he braked to a stop outside the door, the fumes from the exhaust caught up with him creating a halo of smoke that followed him through the door and into the waiting lounge. A small girl screamed at the sight of Maratse, blood streaking his hands and face, and a sharp glint in his eye. A young woman enveloped the girl in her arms as Maratse took another step and glared at the passengers preparing to board the Dash.

"That's quite an entrance," Petra said, as she pushed back her chair and shouldered her pack.

"What?" Maratse twitched as she placed her hand on his arm.

"What's wrong?"

"Have you seen her?"

"Seen who?" Petra said, as Maratse stalked between the tables. "David, I just got here. Who are you looking for?"

"Therese Kleinschmidt," he said, and then again, louder, for the benefit of the passengers, personnel, and visitors.

"You're scaring people," Petra said, and slipped her hand down Maratse's arm to take his hand. "And why are you covered in blood?"

"Narwhal," he said, as he pulled free of her grasp. Maratse opened the door to the toilets, and banged on each locked door, shouting Therese's name.

"Okay," Petra said, and dumped her pack on the floor. "That's enough. She gripped Maratse's elbow and steered him behind the check-in desk and into the small office behind it. She shut the door, pushed him into a chair, and tucked her hands onto her hips. "You're lucky I'm in uniform," she said. "Now talk."

"Therese, the German…"

"Yes?"

"She took something from me, something I took from the man on the ice."

"The one who killed the two crew members?"

"Maybe. Dieter. He had a journal, and I took it from him."

"A journal?" Petra gripped the back of an office chair and pulled it in front of Maratse. She sat down. "Alfred Wegener's journal?"

"Maybe." Maratse shrugged. "It was old and written in German. I couldn't read it," he said, and looked at Petra.

"And you thought Therese was leaving on the plane?"

"It made sense." He glanced at the door.

"She's not here." Petra ran her fingers through her hair, tugging at her pony tail as she thought.

Maratse tapped his bloody nails on his knees, looked at Petra, and said, "It's good to see you, Piitalaat."

She laughed. "It is good to see you too, although, the way you barged through the door, it was pretty wild."

"*Iiji*," he said. Maratse's cheeks twitched and he ran a bloody hand over his wispy beard.

"Do you know what's in the journal?"

"*Eeqqi.*"

"I have an idea, and, if it had been stolen from me, I might have reacted just like you." Petra reached out to touch Maratse's knee. "Why did you take it? Why not give it to Simonsen?"

Maratse shrugged, and said, "I just took it."

"A policeman wouldn't do that."

"I'm retired," he said, and grinned. "But, I thought it might be important, and I thought you could read it." He glanced at the door. "What do we do now?"

"If she's not here, where else would she go? The yacht?"

Maratse shook his head. "I came from there." He lifted his hands to show her the blood-streaked palms. "They were working on the whales on the ice. I didn't see her."

"She must have gone to Uummannaq. Maybe she's trying to talk to the crew."

"She said something about the ship's log, and how she couldn't find it."

"Then one of the crew must have it." Petra stood up. "She's in Uummannaq. Without a doubt."

"Then we can find her." Maratse pushed back his chair. Petra bent over to kiss him on the cheek as he stood up.

"It *is* good to see you," she said, "but now we need to get going."

"You're not dressed for the snowmobile."

"Give me a minute, and I will be." Petra left Maratse alone in the office. He watched her leave, and then loitered at the door.

In truth, he had surprised himself when he took the journal. He had no need for it, but somehow it had seemed important. It was clear it meant a great deal to Dieter, it was the only thing he had on him when they found him. He would ask Petra to ask him, as soon as they got to Uummannaq.

"You're looking for a European woman with red hair?" One of the airport staff said, as she walked into the office.

"*Iiji.*"

"She was here, and then she borrowed a snowmobile."

"*Qujanaq*," Maratse said, and waited for Petra.

She appeared a few minutes later wearing thick ski salopettes the colour of blushed mango. She zipped the sides beneath her black police jacket and nodded that she was ready. She tucked her arms inside the backpack, sat on the snowmobile and then circled her hands around Maratse's waist as he climbed into the driver's position.

Petra spoke in his ear as he started the engine. "No cigarette?"

"I'm trying to quit," he said, and reversed away from the airport building, before clicking the snowmobile into first gear and driving down the hill to the ice. The skids bumped over the ice foot, and Maratse accelerated towards the white peaks of the heart-shaped mountain that gave Uummannaq island and the town its name.

They cruised alongside the tracks carved by the taxis, police cars, and the ambulance that had driven between Uummannaq and the mainland, once the ice had been declared safe to drive on. Petra rested her head on Maratse's shoulder, content to observe the winter landscape, so very different from a few months earlier, when the sea was exposed, along with the evil that drove some men to seek power, and to be consumed by it. She spared a thought for Tinka, the daughter of Greenland's first minister, and the circumstances of her last case in the area.

"You're quiet," Maratse said, as he slowed at the mouth of the harbour.

"Just thinking."

Maratse drove up the ramp to the right of the boats and a dog team tethered on the ice beside a bloody sledge. He drove down the road to the hospital, and parked outside. He turned off the engine as Petra climbed off the snowmobile and adjusted the straps on her back.

"Does Simonsen know you are here?"

"He knows I'm on my way," she said. "He said I should call him from the hospital."

"He'll meet you here?"

"Yes."

Maratse nodded. "Then I'll try and find Therese." He climbed onto the snowmobile. It stuttered into life after three turns of the key. "Needs more fuel," he said when Petra frowned. "Dieter is bound to be in the hospital still. You stay here and speak to him and I'll ask Danielsen to take me to the other members of the crew – the survivors. They are not behind bars, but they have not been allowed to leave. Danielsen will tell me where they are."

"I'll need to talk to them too."

"*Iiji*," Maratse said, "but Dieter first."

"Why?"

"Because I don't know if he'll live. He had a knife in his belly when I found him." Maratse backed the snowmobile until he was positioned right beside Petra. "Talk to him first."

Maratse waited for Petra to go inside and then pulled out of the hospital parking area, and drove up the hill, past the blue offices of Nukissiorfiit, the power company, and further up the hill to the police station on the right. Danielsen grinned when he saw Maratse's hands.

"Narwhal?"

"*Iiji.*"

"Christmas is saved, eh?" Danielsen stood up. "What do you need?"

"Petra is here. She's going to meet Simonsen at the hospital."

"He's on his way, and then maybe I get the car for an hour or so."

"It must be difficult with only one car."

"That's not the worst; my CDs were in the one that sank." Danielsen lifted the flap of the counter and nodded for Maratse to follow him. "You want to talk to the crew?"

"I'm probably not allowed."

"You can be a guest. It's allowed. But why do you want to talk to them."

"You remember the German girl?" Maratse waited as Danielsen said something about Therese's looks and temperament. He raised his eyebrows in agreement, and said, "She left my house earlier, and I think she came here."

"Of course," Danielsen said, "she must think the crew has what she wants."

"How do you know?"

"I watched her pull the yacht apart, remember?"

"She also has a journal, the one they were looking for."

"Wegener's journal? How does she have that?"

"Because I took it from Dieter," Maratse said. He shrugged at the look Danielsen gave him, and said, "When I searched him for a weapon."

"And you think she has it?"

"*Iiji*, and Petra says it is important."

Danielsen took his jacket off the rack by the door and pulled it on, adjusting the waistband to free the grip of the pistol on his hip. He noticed when Maratse glanced at it. "*Naamik*, you can't have it." Maratse opened the door and gestured for Danielsen to get on the back of the snowmobile. The engine spluttered into life. Maratse turned in the parking area and pulled out onto the road.

"Where are the crew staying?"

"In the old youth hostel. The council bought it from the hotel owner. We put them there."

Maratse nodded and drove up the hill, turned left and accelerated past the fire station, passing the old police house on the rocks above the road, and then along the upper road through the village. He reduced speed when a group of children ran across the road to the store. Maratse slowed into the next bend and then accelerated to the hostel.

Danielsen tapped him on the shoulder and pointed at a woman getting onto a snowmobile parked under the hostel's staircase. "The hair," he said, and waited for Maratse to react to the shock of red hair flowing out from beneath the woman's helmet and across the shoulders of her jacket. Even in the dark of early afternoon, there was no mistaking Therese. She turned as she started the engine, her head fixed in their direction as she recognised Maratse. Therese flipped the visor into position, revved the engine, and gripped the handlebars as the snowmobile lurched forwards.

"On or off?" Maratse shouted.

"I'm staying on," Danielsen said. "Go get her."

Maratse twisted the throttle and thundered down the hill, past the hostel on the right. Therese's snowmobile slipped on a swathe of ice outside a water station. She recovered, and sped up a hill cut into the mountain with steep rock walls on both sides. Maratse slid across the same patch of ice, and followed her.

"We're high above the sea here," Danielsen said, as Maratse braked into a hard left as Therese raced between two dog teams, snow pluming from the track churning beneath her seat. "But if she gets to the end of the road, there's a narrow path that zigzags between the rocks." Danielsen pointed. "There," he said. "She must know about it."

"She's been here before."

"She must have been." Danielsen tapped Maratse's shoulder.

"What."

"It's steep."

"Okay."

They heard the change in engine tone as Therese braked to navigate the sharp turns to the left, and the sharper turns to the right, as she snaked the snowmobile between the rocks and down to the sea ice below. Maratse followed, invigorated by the chase, as eager and reckless to catch Therese as she was to escape. He accelerated when she bumped the snowmobile off the island and onto the ice.

"Go," Danielsen shouted, as Maratse throttled up, and twisted the skids with two quick jerks onto the ice to follow the path Therese carved through the fresh snow that had fallen in the night. The red rear light of Therese's snowmobile, almost as vivid as her hair, glowed like the eye of the devil as she topped one hundred kilometres per hour, pushing the snowmobile towards one hundred and fifty.

Maratse felt the bite of the air on his ears, his cheeks, the tip of his nose. He pushed on, chasing the eye of the devil. He felt Danielsen shift his grip, clutching him tighter around his waist.

"Hold on," Maratse said.

He accelerated.

Maratse knew the location of the leads he was forced to work around close to the mainland, and he also knew the current ran strongest closer to the island. Therese, he noticed, favoured the perceived safety of the island and hugged the coastline, whereas Maratse drifted away from the island, and further out. The advantage Therese gained by gunning the snowmobile along the island, would, he gambled, be lost once she encountered bad ice, and had to slow down.

"There," Danielsen said, and pointed. "She's slowing."

Maratse grinned, as he turned in a wide arc towards Therese, but as she slowed to negotiate thinner ice, the engine started to splutter, and they lost speed.

"Fuel?" Danielsen said, as he released his grip around Maratse's waist.

"*Iiji.*"

The engine coughed to a stop, thrusting them into a quiet bubble of sound defined by the grating of the skids on the ice as the snowmobile slid to a halt. Maratse reached for the packet of cigarettes in his pocket and offered one to Danielsen. They smoked in silence as they watched Therese pick her way across the ice, away from the poorer surface eroded by the current beneath.

"She's going to get away," Danielsen said. "But where will she go?"

Maratse said nothing. He knew where she was going.

Therese stopped and let the engine idle. There was just thirty metres between them. It might as well have been three hundred. She unclipped the strap of the helmet and lifted it from her head. Therese placed the helmet in front of her, ruffled her hair with gloved fingers, and then stopped to wave at the two men.

"She's playing with us."

"*Iiji.*"

Maratse pictured the flush of red in her cheeks as her skin cooled. He saw her freckles – so many – her red hair, those green eyes. He felt a flush of heat when he remembered seeing her for the first time wearing nothing more than his dirty bath towel that barely reached her thighs. She was a beauty, he knew that, but there was a beast driving her, and he knew too, that he would have to be smarter if he was going to catch her. And he would need more fuel.

"The navy," he said, as Therese pulled the helmet onto her head, adjusted her position, and revved the engine.

"What's that?"

"Maybe the navy can catch her."

Maratse rolled the cigarette between his teeth and placed a warm palm against his cheek. He dipped his head at Therese as she waved. He heard the click of gears and then she was gone, accelerating into the polar night.

"She is going to the *Ophelia,*" Maratse said.

"The yacht?"

"That's how she is getting out of Greenland."

Danielsen tugged his phone out of his pocket, and said, "She must be crazy to sail alone in winter."

"*Iiji.*" Maratse said as Danielsen called Simonsen. He listened as the young constable briefed the Uummannaq Chief of Police, and watched as the tail light of Therese's snowmobile blinked with each bump in the ice.

Danielsen finished the call, and said, "Simonsen says he'll call Ilulissat, see if they can intercept her. She's sailing away with our crime scene."

Maratse remembered what he had read about the *Ophelia*, what the boat was capable of. He recalled the pictures of the *Ophelia* locked in the ice in Arctic and Antarctic waters. Given what the boat was designed to do, all it needed was a capable and adventurous skipper. From what he knew of Therese Kleinschmidt, the Greenlandic police, even the Danish Navy, would be hard-pressed to catch her.

"Simonsen is sending someone to pick us up. He wants us both at the hospital. The German guy, Dieter, has started talking."

Chapter 15

Dieter tried to blink his eyes open. He was in a bed, a real one, not a broken cot in a hunter's cabin. The fabric he could feel with his fingertips was cotton, not wool stiff with mould. It was sore when he moved. He kept trying to open his eyes, turning his head in the direction of the sounds – a scrape of a chair leg perhaps, maybe even voices. He sensed there were people waiting for him to open them, and the minute he did so, he would have to answer some hard questions.

"I need to open my eyes," Dieter said, his words morphine-slurred.

The woman's face was as unexpected as it was angelic, lit as it was in the soft light of the bedside lamp. She smiled at him, and Dieter squinted at her. She spoke his language, and he blinked again to focus.

"Take your time," she said. "There's plenty of time."

"Who are you?"

"My name is Sergeant Petra Jensen," she said. "I'm with the Greenland Police."

"Am I under arrest?"

Dieter rubbed his eyes with his fingers, and focussed on the policewoman sitting beside his bed.

"You're not under arrest, not yet, but I do need to ask you some questions."

"Who's that?" Dieter asked, and looked at the man leaning against the wall.

"He's the chief of police here in Uummannaq. His name is Simonsen."

"Have we met?"

Simonsen nodded, and said, "I pulled you out of a sinking car."

Dieter concentrated on the man's words, which were not quite as clear as the woman's German, not as practised. But the image of the car sinking through the ice seemed familiar.

He heard the shush of black water sluicing into the car, pushing at the mats and the carpet hiding the wiring, the metal shell, the bolts and welded joints. He heard the shouts of the policeman, the rising panic in the man's voice, and he felt the press of another man as he crawled over Dieter's body to tug at the door. There was a sense of urgency about the man, but Dieter remembered him being calm, and it was a similar feeling that flooded through his own body, dampening the pain from the knife sticking out of his stomach, a liquid darkness washing through his body as the police car sank beneath the ice.

"I remember," Dieter said.

"That's good," Petra said. "Now, if we work back from there. What else do you remember?"

Dieter sniffed at the strange smell he imagined was coming from the wound in his stomach. He looked from the police chief to the sergeant, and then reached for the glass of water by his bed. Petra helped him take a sip. He licked at the flakes of skin on his lips and then spoke.

"I stole a police car. I was trying to get away."

"From who?"

"Not who, *what*. I wanted to get away from the yacht, from the *Ophelia*."

"What were you doing on the yacht?"

"I was trying to find something." Dieter glanced at Simonsen, and said, "The policeman, the one in plain clothes, he caught me going through my bags in the cabin. I was hiding in the cabin, that's when I heard him come in."

"And what did you do?"

"I wanted to get out. I felt trapped, so I grabbed a knife, the kind we wear on our belts when on deck. I think I cut him when I slashed at him, and then we fell – we slipped, I think … on blood." Dieter paused as Petra made a note with a pencil in her notepad. He waited for her to look up. "We fell, and the knife went into my stomach."

"But you kept going?"

"Yes, I had to get away from the yacht."

"Why?"

"Because I couldn't let them have it."

"Have what?"

"The journal. Wegener's journal."

Dieter waited as Petra said something to Simonsen. It had been a long time since he had spoken Danish, but he understood the woods for *book* and *stolen* and something about a man called Maratse.

"Sergeant," Dieter said, "where is the journal?"

"Why don't you tell us why it is so important?"

"You don't have it?" Dieter tried to sit up, but the pain in his stomach forced him to lie down again.

"We know where it is."

Dieter closed his eyes, and said, "The journal is a record of Alfred Wegener's explorations of Svartenhuk. It includes his findings, and information about the samples he took, and where."

"What samples?"

"Thorium."

Dieter opened his eyes at the sound of Petra's

pencil scratching the surface of the paper in her pad. He waited for her to stop.

"You said you didn't want *them* to have the journal. Who is *them* and why shouldn't they have it?"

The light in the room brightened as a nurse opened the door. Dieter watched as Petra waved her away. The door closed, and he relaxed into the dim light cast by the lamp at his bedside. It reminded him of the flames licking at the thick glass window in the door of the cabin stove.

"I was hired for the expedition as an expert on Alfred Wegener," Dieter said.

"Are you?"

"Yes. I have worked at several institutions. Berndt found me through a contact of his at the Alfred Wegener Institution at Bremerhaven."

"And Berndt is?"

"Aleksander Berndt is the CEO of the Berndt Media Group. He is also the owner of *Ophelia*. It is his step-daughter who runs *Ophelia Expeditions*."

"Therese Kleinschmidt?" asked Simonsen.

"Yes, exactly."

Dieter continued. "I was flattered to be asked to join the expedition, and excited. The chance to find and recover one of Alfred Wegener's lost journals was too good to miss."

"So you said yes?"

"At once, at the first meeting."

"And the journal you found was the one you had hoped to find?"

"Yes." Dieter took another sip of water as Petra made a note. "It was a bit of a disappointment, really. The journal was exactly where we thought it would be."

"In the cabin?"

Dieter nodded. "We asked local hunters many times if they knew of the cabin, and, if they did, if they had seen a journal, but they said nothing. I was worried they might have burned the journal to start a fire."

"But they didn't."

"A Danish hunter – I think he was called Axel – told the captain he knew where the cabin was. She paid him for the information, and she was going to pay him to take us there, but I don't know what happened after that."

"What do you mean?"

"I mean that we prepared to leave the boat – five of us. The captain would stay behind. But the hunter did not show. At least, not before we left. I don't know if he came later." Dieter gritted his teeth as a wave of pain flashed through his body.

"This was when you skied across the sea ice to the mountains?"

"To Svartenhuk, yes."

"Did you find the cabin?"

"Not at first. We were caught out in a wind blowing down the mountain. There was a lot of snow. The team wanted to go back. Nele was the guide, but Henrik was leading the team. He said we should turn around."

"And did you?"

"Not me. I knew we were close, and if they had listened to me, we would have found the cabin together."

"So you stayed on the mountain?"

"Yes."

"And found the cabin?"

"Just. It was difficult."

"But no-one can prove you were in the cabin,"

Simonsen said.

"I found the journal. That is proof."

"But no-one saw you."

Petra frowned at Simonsen, but the chief of police held up his hand, waited for Dieter to answer.

"I called my wife, on the satellite phone."

"From the cabin?"

"Yes."

Petra asked for the telephone number and Dieter gave it to her. "Remember the country code," he said, "forty-nine."

Petra tapped the pencil on the page. "So the team returned to the *Ophelia*, and you found the cabin, found the journal, and then went back to the yacht."

"Yes."

"But when you went on board..."

"It was empty. Everyone was gone. Just lots of dogs on the ice. And then the policemen came."

"Dogs?"

"Hunters' dogs," Simonsen said. "The narwhal came down from Upernavik."

Petra nodded. "But you didn't think it was strange that the yacht was empty? I thought they were supposed to wait for you."

"I didn't think about it," Dieter said.

"Because you wanted to find something," Petra said, as she flipped through her notes.

"Yes, a thumb drive."

"Like a USB?"

"Yes."

"What was on it?"

"A backup of my notes. I scanned them into my computer before leaving Berlin."

"And they are important?"

"Most important, especially now."

"Why?"

"Because a man came to my house, and took the notes from Marlene." Dieter glanced at Simonsen. "She told me when we talked on the satellite phone. She said the man needed the notes to help find me, and to help me."

"With what?"

"This," Dieter said, with a wave of his hand. He grimaced, and pushed his head back onto the pillow. When he spoke again it was barely more than a whisper. Dieter caught the faint trace of Petra's perfume as she leaned over him to hear what he said. "When I was invited to join the expedition, I was given a list of the other members, and a brief contact sheet with details about their careers and educations. When I searched for the same people online, I found different photos, but the same names. The dates and degrees were correct, but some of the specialist areas were slightly off."

"In what way?"

"Geology instead of geography. Marine science not meteorology."

"Why does it matter?"

"When you read Wegener's journal, it matters."

"Tell me."

Dieter looked into the sergeant's eyes, and said, "Wegener found thorium in the mountains, a lot of it, but it was never reported, when he lost his journal it was forgotten, and when he died, the secret was buried with him."

"And a geologist?" Petra asked.

"Would be far more interested in minerals than a geographer."

"Marine scientists…"

"They look down at the seabed, meteorologists

look up."

"What did you think they were going to do with the journal?" Simonsen asked, as she took a step closer to Dieter's hospital bed.

"After being scanned, it would be preserved, papers would be written, and I could move Marlene into a nice house on the outskirts of the city, perhaps even to Bremerhaven."

"You could advance your career?"

"Yes, Sergeant, a find like this is priceless."

"You would get paid more?"

"Maybe, that's not important. But I could have my pick of jobs. Maybe even teach abroad."

Dieter closed his eyes. He heard his name being called, twice. He blinked and focussed on the police sergeant standing by his bed.

"Dieter," she said, "two people were murdered on board *Ophelia*. Henrik Nielsen and Antje Jung."

"Murdered?"

"Yes. You remember the blood?"

"Yes," he said, and lifted his head. "I was focussed on the thumb drive. I needed to prove my theory."

"Which is?"

"Berndt didn't want the journal, he wanted Wegener's secret."

"But Berndt picked the team."

"Yes."

"So he knew about the fake references?"

"Maybe he didn't," Simonsen said. He placed his hand on the rail at the foot of the bed, and said, "Nele Schneider says you and she were having an affair. Is that correct?"

"What?"

"She also said that the two deceased, Nielsen and

Jung, were romantically involved."

"I don't remember," Dieter said.

"Don't, or can't?"

"Chief," Petra said.

"I have a wife in Berlin," Dieter said. "Marlene and I are very happy together. We want to have children."

"Were you having an affair?"

Dieter looked at Petra. He shifted position, wincing at the pain in his stomach. "*Ophelia* can be quite cramped, intimate," he said. "We sailed from Germany. It took a long time. We all got to know each other, some more than others." Dieter took Petra's hand, and said, "I have been unfaithful, just one time, on *Ophelia*."

"With Nele Schneider?"

Dieter shook his head.

"Who?"

"The captain. Katharina Fischer. Just one night, when we were in Ilulissat, before we sailed to the edge of the ice."

The door opened and Dieter let go of Petra's hand. The nurse entered the room with a bedpan, a thermometer and a sleeve to check his blood pressure. She waved the police officers out of the room, and pressed the thermometer into Dieter's ear.

Dieter watched her as she worked, listed to the click and clack of her pen as she recorded his temperature on the chart hanging from his bed, and then pressed the pen into the metal coil holding it in place in the breast pocket of her uniform. He could see the police sergeant watching him from the corridor. He tried to smile, but the nurse blocked his view as she took his blood pressure, pumping the sleeve around his arm until it was tight, almost uncomfortable. Another click of the pen, and then she asked him something in English, he knew it was important, but not as urgent as his confession to the policewoman. He needed to tell her that he loved Marlene. He needed to tell Marlene, but the nurse was insistent. She placed the bedpan by the side of his bed, and then rolled back the sheets to look at the bandage plastered to his abdomen. He smelled it then, as she peeled back the plaster and released a whiff of decay, bacteria, something hot and active in his wound. Dieter started to sweat. The room dimmed, and he heard the clap of the nurse's feet as she walked to the door and called out something in Greenlandic. A doctor arrived at Dieter's bedside. It was time for Dieter to dig in and focus on recovering from his wound.

"For Marlene," he whispered, and closed his eyes.

Chapter 16

Petra tugged the collar of her police jacket around her neck and walked outside. She found Simonsen smoking beside the police Toyota. He flicked the butt of his cigarette onto the ground and scuffed it into a patch of ice with the toe of his boot. Petra stuffed her hands into her jacket pockets and waited for Simonsen to speak. The burr of a snowmobile across the hard-packed snow covering the road distracted her, and she caught the eye of the driver, a grizzled Dane with what looked like a permanent sneer scarred into his top lip. Petra held his gaze until the man turned his head and accelerated up the road towards the ramp leading down to the sea ice.

"About time," Simonsen said. "He's been in town far too long."

"Who is he?"

"Axel Stein."

"The *Axel* Dieter mentioned?"

"Yep."

"Then why are we not interviewing him?"

"Danielsen spoke to Axel when he was in hospital. He cut his own arm with a knife."

"A knife?" Petra took a step towards the car as Axel weaved between the dogs and the fishing boats locked in the sea ice.

"Forget it, Sergeant. Axel isn't the killer."

"He has an alibi?"

"He told Danielsen that he was approached by

one of the crew – he couldn't remember which one. They called his mobile and he talked to them for about three minutes before hanging up. His phone log shows the call, from a German mobile."

"And there's nothing strange about that?"

"The strange thing is that he had a mobile at all. Axel has taken a hunter's cabin and called it his own. He has a history of alcohol and abuse. Children are frightened of him, especially when their parents tell stories about the *Stein Monster*. It suits Axel just fine. He'll die in that cabin."

"What makes you so sure he didn't kill the crew?"

"Axel is an evil man, there's no doubt, but he's also a coward. He wouldn't fight a man. Besides, this is too sophisticated for him."

"In what way?"

"The way the crew were drugged. Axel couldn't figure that out. He's more of a blunt-force-trauma than anything fancy. Although," Simonsen said, with a glance at the shadow of Axel Stein disappearing across the ice, "I didn't expect him to stay so long in town. I'll have Danielsen look into it." Simonsen nudged Petra's arm and pointed at a taxi bumping across the ice, up the ramp, and along the road to the hospital. "Here he is now."

The taxi driver waved as Danielsen and Maratse opened the doors and stepped out of the car. Maratse took a can of fuel from the car boot, and gave the driver a few hundred kroner. The smile on Maratse's face tugged at his cheeks as he walked over to join Petra and Simonsen. He put the jerry can on the ground by his feet as Danielsen leaned against the side of the police car.

"Our brave knights," Simonsen said, with a quick glance at Danielsen.

"We screwed up, Chief," he said.

"You did. Now how about you make up for it and go inside the hospital. You can warm up while you wait outside the German's door."

Danielsen looked at his watch, and said, "My shift's nearly over."

"I know, I'll send one of the assistants to relieve you."

Danielsen nodded, winked at Petra, and then walked inside the hospital.

Simonsen waited until the door closed with a thump, and then said, "You ran out of fuel?"

"*Iiji.*"

"Well, she shouldn't get far. The navy has the *Ejnar Mikkelsen* just south of Ilulissat. They'll find her." Simonsen nodded at the car, and said, "Get in."

"Where are we going?" Maratse asked.

"To talk to the crew," Petra said. She climbed into the passenger seat as Maratse put the fuel can in the boot and got in behind Simonsen. Petra caught Maratse's eye in the rear-view mirror, and, even in the dark, she was almost certain she saw him blush.

Simonsen backed out of the parking spot, and drove to the hostel where the crew were staying. The moon ducked behind a cloud, and the polar afternoon did its best to pretend it was later than one thought.

There was a crowd outside the youth hostel, a flash of bright blue-tinged beams from smartphones, and a dark patch of something on the snow. One of the crowd ran to the driver's side of the car as Simonsen wound down the window.

"What's going on?"

"Someone is dead."

"Slow down, Angut," Simonsen said, as the man chattered through a description of what happened.

Petra got out of the car, and Maratse followed.

The crowd peeled to both sides as Petra approached. She stopped to look at the blood staining the packed snow on the road, stepped around it, and knelt beside the body on the ground. She pressed her fingers to the man's throat, pulled out her mobile, and called the hospital.

"What did you see?" she asked. When a young woman began to answer in Greenlandic, Petra turned to Maratse for help.

"He fell from the balcony," Maratse translated, pausing as the woman continued. "There was some shouting in the house, women's voices, and then he came out onto the balcony. He might have been pushed. She can't remember, but they did film the fall." Maratse took the phone from the woman's hand and showed it to Petra. The video – barely six seconds long – caught the man halfway into his fall and the sound of the wet crack of his head on the road.

"The fall killed him," Petra said, and looked up at the balcony. "She thinks he might have been pushed?"

"Maybe. She's not sure."

Petra turned at the metallic clap of Simonsen's door. His boots crunched through a shallow drift of snow as he joined them beside the body.

"There's a video," Maratse said, as he turned the screen towards Simonsen.

The Chief of Police nodded, looked at the young Greenlander, and said, "I'll need a copy."

"*Aap*," she said, as Maratse returned her phone.

"You really are a crime magnet," Simonsen whispered to Maratse. He nodded at the balcony surrounding the first floor of the hostel. "Go with Sergeant Jensen." Simonsen caught Petra's eye, and said, "You do the talking, Sergeant."

"Yes, sir."

Each step on the way up to the first floor was caked with a layer of snow-turned-ice. Petra slipped on the deck of the balcony, caught the railing, and looked over the side to the body below.

"He could have just slipped?" she said. Petra waited for Maratse to join her and then knocked on the door.

Petra knocked another three times before a young woman opened the door, her eyes widened as she recognised Maratse.

"It's you," she said in English, "the hunter on the yacht."

Petra glanced at Maratse, and then pushed gently at the door. "Can we come in?"

"Yes."

Maratse banged the snow from his boots and followed Petra inside the hostel. There were four rooms spaced evenly around a central living area. Petra touched Maratse's elbow and nodded at two empty bottles of wine on the kitchen counter. They followed the woman into the lounge area where another woman was sprawled on the sofa.

"Katharina," said the young German, shaking the woman gently. "It's the police."

Katharina took a long breath and turned on the sofa, clutching the cushioned arm with thin fingers as if it was a railing on the *Ophelia*, as if they were crashing through waves, and their guests were obstacles to be avoided. She leaned back and pointed at Maratse. "Who is he?"

"His name is Maratse, and I'm Sergeant Jensen. When did you start drinking?"

Katharina sighed, and said, "Early. What else is there to do?"

"Is it just the two of you?"

"No," said the young woman. "Our friend, Abraham – he just went to the bathroom."

"And what is your name?"

"Nele Schneider."

"I'm sorry to tell you this, but your friend is dead," Petra said. "He fell from the balcony."

"What?" Nele started towards the door, but Maratse stepped in front of her.

"We need you to answer some questions," Petra said, as Maratse helped Nele onto the sofa.

"More questions?" Katharina said. "All we do is answer questions."

"Your friend just died. I'm sure you want to help us find out how, and why?"

"Not without a lawyer," Katharina said. She took Nele's hand. "Don't say anything."

Petra unzipped her jacket and pulled her notebook from the cargo pocket in her trousers. She sat down on a chair opposite the two women. Maratse retreated to the kitchen to wait.

"You're the captain of the *Ophelia*," Petra said, and looked at Katharina. "Surely you can answer that."

The woman shrugged, and said, "Yes."

"And you're one of the crew?"

"Yes," Nele said, "I'm the mountaineer." She fidgeted on the sofa and glanced at the door.

"The mountaineer?"

"The one with the climbing and skiing skills. That's why I'm on the expedition." Nele started to stand up. "I want to see him."

"A few more questions, first," Petra said. She heard the captain whisper something in German, and Petra made a note, something about *too many deaths*.

"Abraham is our friend," Nele said. "We really must see him."

"His body will be taken to the hospital. I'll arrange for you to see him soon, until then, I need to know when he was last with you?"

"Twenty minutes, maybe," Nele said. She looked at the captain, and said, "You remember?"

"Not without a lawyer."

Petra switched to Danish and asked Maratse to fetch Simonsen. She looked at her watch, turned back to the captain, and said, "The time is seventeen minutes past five, and I'm arresting you on suspicion of being party to the death of Abraham Baumann."

"You can't prove anything," Katharina said, as Petra removed a pair of handcuffs from her belt.

"Not without a lawyer, apparently." She tugged the woman to her feet, pulled her hands behind her back, and snapped the metal bracelets around her wrists. She pointed at the sofa and ordered the younger woman to sit and wait as she walked the captain to the door. Simonsen met her on the balcony and Petra let him take her down the stairs.

"Refusing to cooperate?" Simonsen said.

"Yes," Petra said. "She wants a lawyer."

"That'll take some time." He caught the woman as she slipped. "Careful now, I can't have two dead bodies in one night; the doctor will never forgive me."

Petra waited until Simonsen opened the rear passenger door of the police car, and helped the woman onto the seat. He waved just before driving off in the direction of the police station. Petra closed the door to the hostel and joined Maratse at the railing of the balcony.

"He's letting you stick around," she said, with a nod towards the police car.

"I think he feels guilty."

"For being mean to you?"

"For nearly drowning me."

"That's right," Petra said. "You need to tell me more about that sometime."

"I'm okay, Piitalaat."

"I'm glad," she said, and curled her hand around his arm. Petra leaned her head against Maratse's shoulder for a second, and then pulled free. She nodded at the door. "Are you coming?"

"*Iiji.*"

Nele hadn't moved from the sofa. Her legs were tucked beneath her bottom. She had wrapped a blanket over her knees. Petra sat down opposite her, while Maratse stayed in the kitchen. The young woman looked at him for a moment, and then turned her attention to Petra.

"I'm happy to answer any questions," she said.

"That's good." Petra opened her notebook.

"But not about Abraham. I don't know how he fell. I just remember him going outside. That's all."

"Was he drunk?"

"Yes."

"And you didn't hear anything?"

"No," Nele said. She looked at the floor. "We were shouting. We didn't hear anything."

"We?"

"The captain and me."

"What were you shouting about?"

Nele lifted her head, slowly, as if she was pulling against something that was wrapped around her neck. When her eyes were level with Petra's, she said, "It was about Therese. She was here earlier. She took something from the captain."

Petra heard Maratse fidget in the kitchen. She

lifted her pencil from the page of her notepad. "What did she take?"

"A thumb drive. You know, a mini hard drive?"

"I know what it is," Petra said, "but why is it important?"

"The ship's log," Maratse said, as he walked out of the kitchen to stand beside Petra.

Nele shook her head. "That's not important. It was something else. I'm not sure, but I think it was files of some kind. Documents."

"Did the thumb drive belong to the captain?"

"No."

"Who then?"

"I think it was Dieter's."

Petra reached over the arm of the chair and tapped Maratse's leg. He found a chair in the kitchen and carried it into the living room area. The woman watched him as he sat down beside Petra.

"I have one more question," Petra said.

"Okay." Nele shifted position, and then smoothed the blanket over her legs. The sofa sighed as she moved.

"Were you having an affair with Dieter?"

Nele flicked her head towards Maratse, and then pressed the tip of her nail against her lip. "No," she said, her eyes locked on Maratse's.

"You told Simonsen that you were."

"I was covering for the captain." Nele gripped the arm of the sofa and looked at Petra.

"Okay, Nele. Just stay there."

Petra closed her notebook and nodded for Maratse to join her in the kitchen. She filled the kettle with water and switched it on. She leaned on the counter and watched the girl from the kitchen as the kettle boiled. When the water started to bubble and spit, she switched to Danish and spoke quietly to Maratse.

"The thumb drive is Dieter's. He said his notes include scans of documents that prove the crew of the *Ophelia* are not who they claim to be."

Maratse leaned against the counter, crossed his arms across his chest, and said, "Therese has the journal and the USB drive. What will she do with them?"

Petra shrugged. "Destroy them. Toss them overboard. Dieter said that somebody collected a box of notes from his house, that the USB was a backup. He scanned the documents."

Maratse turned his back on Nele. He leaned close to Petra's ear. "You know I'm not good with computers, but I do know that he had to scan something onto the computer before copying it to a USB."

"And if they didn't take the computer…"

"There will be a copy on the hard drive." Maratse grinned, and said, "I like it when you smile, Piitalaat."

"I like it when you talk about computers."

"Because it makes me sound smarter than I am?"

Flecks of light from the kitchen danced in Petra's eyes. "No," she said, and hid her mouth with her hand. "But I like the serious pinch of skin you have, right there." Petra pressed her finger into the centre of Maratse's forehead.

The lid of the kettle flapped as the water boiled. Petra brushed past Maratse and found clean mugs in the cupboard. She made coffee with instant granules from a jar on the counter. Maratse picked up two mugs, and took a step towards the living room area.

"Wait," Petra whispered.

"*Iiji?*"

"How do you feel about going to Berlin?"

Maratse wrinkled his nose.

"Oh, come on, it will be fun."

"Why, Piitalaat?"

"Because it might be the only way to prove who has done what in this case." She paused. "You want to find the murderer, don't you?"

"I'm retired," he said, and shrugged.

"Not from where I'm standing."

Chapter 17

Therese had never seen a blood floe, neither was she prepared for the thick stench of intestines that washed over the fleece tube around her neck, soaking into the soft fibres like oil. The skids at the front of the snowmobile rattled over globs of frozen blood as Therese slowed on her approach to the *Ophelia*. She turned off the engine, and the last rumble of the motor was lost in the vast black sky and even blacker sea beyond the ice. Therese slid the visor up and over the front of the helmet and clawed at the straps. If she thought she could escape the bloody, heady smell of dead whale, she was mistaken. She dumped the helmet on the ice, gagged her way to the ladder, and climbed onto the deck of her father's yacht.

"Stepfather," she said, as she looked down upon the bloody ice, and wondered what he would think of it. He would say *quotas* when she cried *butchery*, say *subsistence* to counter her *slaughter*, but either way he would be impressed, it was hard not to be.

Another thing that impressed Therese was the fact that the *Ophelia* was untouched. Apart from traces of the police, she could see no sign that anyone else other than the expedition crew had been on board. Therese opened the hatch and climbed down into the cockpit. She caught the same smell of blood, but the lack of bloody organs and the cool temperature presented her palate with a more tempered smell, something she intended to clean up as soon as she was underway.

Therese checked the generator, switched on the battery, and started the *Ophelia*'s engine. The lights flickered as the big, sturdy, diesel engine fired and sent the first rumbles of irritation through the hull.

"I know, baby," Therese said. "Soon."

Therese climbed on deck, checked the lines and shrouds, thumped the ice from the decks with the stubborn handle of a broom, and kicked the jagged clumps over the side. The ice was so thick it reminded her of toffee, hammered into assorted pieces to be boxed, sold, and sucked until the edges smoothed and the caramel slid down one's throat. If she tried hard enough Therese could almost imagine the smell of warm toffee, could almost ignore the smell of whale intestines.

When she was done with the deck, and the lines were free of rime ice, Therese bashed the railings with a heavy rubber mallet, flicking her gaze once in a while to the sea ice, searching for headlights.

"If they use dogs, I won't even hear them," she said, her words misting in the light from the *Ophelia*'s deck lights. "I have to get going."

Therese worked her way around the deck, secured the mallet and the broom, and then climbed back onto the ice to free the *Ophelia* from her wintry berth. The ice axes were buried deep and she decided to leave them. Therese returned to the deck, and released the yacht with a few swift saws of her knife through the stiff rope wound through the cleats. She knew the *Ophelia* was well-equipped and tossed the ends of the rope onto the ice. Therese moved quickly across the deck, rolled the ladder into place and slipped the safety wires across the gap to complete the rail running around the deck.

She stopped for a second to listen to the sound of

the engine, freeing her ears from her fleece hat, tilting and twisting her head for anomalies. It all sounded good, exactly as she had left it.

Therese dropped down through the hatch, wrinkled her nose and adjusted the thermostat as the temperature in the cabin rose. She didn't have time to clean, not yet, but neither did she want the *Ophelia*'s interior to compete with the cloying cabbage smell of the ice. She jogged down to the forward cabins, tucked the journal and thumb drive into a small locker next to the toilet, and pulled her personal kit out of stowage below the starboard bunk. Therese pulled off her outdoor gear, added a second mid-layer of thermals, before pulling on her insulated sailing suit. She checked the pockets for extra gloves, hats, and fleece tubes, before securing the trouser cuffs over her boots and zipping the suit to her neck. She twisted her fiery hair beneath a thick fleece hat on her way through the cockpit and onto the deck. The moon flickered between grey clouds pregnant with snow as she pulled on a thin pair of gloves, before stabbing the GPS unit into life and plotting her waypoints. A quick glance at the ice suggested she had plenty of time, and she relaxed.

The course to Ilulissat was familiar. Therese couldn't remember just how many times she had sailed it this past year, but the shifting bergs and the merciless winds and waves that toyed with craft of all sizes on the west coast of Greenland, made waypoints more like guidelines. She would have to be vigilant, again, and be patient, *again*, as the journey would take longer than expected.

It always did.

Therese finished plotting her course, checked the fuel levels, wind levels, pressure levels, and battery levels on the screen, punching them with the stubby tips of her gloved fingers, before taking a last look on the port and starboard sides of the deck. The ice brushing against the front half of the *Ophelia*, from the tip of the bow and another two metres towards the stern, was white, opaque in the glare of her head torch. She returned to the starboard wheel, clicked into reverse gear and throttled the *Ophelia* into the black sea.

Once free of the ice, Therese turned the thirty-six metre long expedition yacht in a slow arc until the bow was aligned with the first of the waypoints glowing green on the screen in front of her. Therese decided to run on diesel until she was free of the rocky tip of the Uummannaq peninsula, where she might find some favourable winds and save on fuel. The course set, and the autopilot engaged, Therese ducked into the cockpit, grabbed a handful of chocolate bars from the kitchen, the satellite phone from the wall mount, and then killed the cockpit lights on her way back onto the deck. She switched off the navigation and running lights as soon as she was back at the wheel.

Therese's green eyes reflected the GPS glare, and she blinked once, before dimming the screen. She unwrapped and stuffed a chocolate bar into her mouth, chewing as she pulled on a second pair of gloves and tightened the draw cord of her hood around her neck. Therese clipped a safety line from the belt at her waist into a D hook behind the wheel, sat down on the chair and switched on the satellite phone. She was still chewing when her stepfather answered her call.

"I've got it, Daddy," she said.

"The thumb drive?"

"Yes." Therese giggled and waited for her father

to react.

"You're laughing?"

"Yes."

"You've got the journal too, haven't you?"

"I have."

Therese smiled at the sound of Aleksander Berndt thumping the desk in his Berlin office.

"But you haven't read it?"

"Not yet, Daddy, I've been busy."

"And the crew?"

"I gave the captain her instructions. The police should have plenty to occupy them for the time being."

"And Dieter?"

"I never saw him. But he is in hospital."

"He'll recover?"

"That's what I heard." Therese waited for her stepfather to finish swearing. "It doesn't matter, Daddy, just print the next article anyway, like we planned."

"I suppose you're right."

"I'll be in Ilulissat before midnight, Greenlandic time, but I have to keep sailing."

"Just long enough to read the journal. You haven't done anything illegal, Therese, don't do anything stupid. All I need is proof, and then you can throw the journal overboard."

"You don't even want to see it? It's a little piece of history."

"The past is only important when shaping the future. Once we own the future, we can rewrite the past. Remember that."

"I will." Therese paused to tap the screen as it dimmed more than she liked. "I have to go, Daddy. Sailor stuff – you know?"

"I know. I want you to take care, and I want you to call me every two hours – earlier if you find the proof in the journal."

"I have to sail. I'm not sure how much I'll be able to read."

"Try."

"Okay," Therese said. A lick of chill wind caught a twist of her hair as she shook her head.

"I can hear you tutting, Therese."

"I'm not."

"It doesn't matter. As long as you realise how important this is."

"I wonder," she said, as another slug of wind, stronger than the last, flapped her hood from her forehead, "would you push Andrea as hard if she could sail."

"That's not fair, Therese. You are both my daughters."

"But only one of us is blood," she whispered.

"Therese?"

"I have to go," she said. "Wind's picking up."

"Call me in two hours."

Therese stabbed the button to end the call, and zipped the phone into her pocket. The light of the moon leaked through a cheesecloth-thin cloud. The filtered glow caught something glinting in the black water some twenty metres in front of the *Ophelia*. Therese unclipped her safety line, and snapped it onto the wire running along the starboard railing. She bent her knees to compensate for the shallow bumps of incoming waves, the first to tease the *Ophelia* since she was released from the ice. When she reached the bow, Therese held onto the railings and squinted into the polar night. The cloud dispersed and the moon lit the pearl-white, cream and ivory tusks of the narwhal as they pierced the surface of the sea. Therese held her breath and watched as the pod of whales swam away from the shore and further out to sea. They must have escaped the hunt, she realised, or slipped past the northerly settlements in the troughs of deep waves, when the moon was hidden, and the snow needled at unprotected eyes.

She wiped at soft needles thumping against her cheeks, catching several in her eyes, blinking, the snow thawed against her eyeballs. The sea was in league with the earth – reluctant to give up its bounty, she thought, or was it Wegener's ghost, making one more attempt to claim his journal and bury the secrets of Svartenhuk at sea?

Therese searched the water ahead. She tried and failed to find the narwhal again. She turned and walked back to the wheel, clipped into the safety lug behind her, and formed the wire-framed hood into a visor to protect her face. The thought of a prolonged battle with the elements encouraged Therese to unclip her safety line, and to duck down into the cockpit. She spent a few minutes boiling water for coffee and draining her bladder before returning to the wheel. She stuffed the flask into a rubber-lined fibreglass tube welded into the deck, pulled on Gore-Tex sailing gauntlets, and squirmed her feet on the deck. She flipped the seat into a high saddle and leaned against it. Therese took the wheel, and let it jerk through her hands with small autopilot adjustments.

"I'm ready," she said, taunting the wind.

There were bergs on the black horizon, black shadowy behemoths, mostly ranged like teeth along the shore. Therese wasn't worried about them, but a chop of thunder began to bother her, and she flicked her head from side to side trying to locate it.

A beam of light, stronger and lower than the moon, cut through the snow swirling above the sea, and Therese realised she had discovered the source of the anonymous thump, in the shape of a Danish Navy Lynx helicopter, most likely from the deck of one of the Thetis-class ships like *HDMS Vædderen* or the smaller Knud Rasmussen-class *HDMS Ejnar Mikkelsen*.

"They've obviously got nothing better to do, eh?" she said.

The *Ophelia* responded with a tug of the wheel. Therese dimmed the screen to the lowest setting, lifted her finger in anticipation of turning the autopilot off, and grinned.

"Now we're sailing." She bit at the snow, licking it from her lips as she grinned. "This is what it's all about."

A childhood memory of stealing her stepsister's favourite t-shirt – the blue one with the rainbow-streaked pony stencilled on the front – and splashing down the muddy lane to the stables, flickered into Therese's mind. She pushed it to one side, and listened for the helicopter, looked for the cone of light from its searchlight, and then remembered once again being chased by her stepfather, the groom, and the stable manager.

She remembered being hunted.

It didn't occur to her at the time, that it was an awful lot of men chasing her for something as silly as a t-shirt. But it didn't seem silly when she heard them cough, wheeze, and swear from running.

Therese had been light on her feet then, quick to climb trees, higher than she should. She hid in the branches of her favourite oak, stayed there until just before the dawn, creeping back to the house with a tattered t-shirt, and twists of moss braided in her hair. Daddy had beaten her the next morning, pulled the t-shirt from her body and thrust her into the shower. Her mother had protested, but he had said something about her leaving if she didn't like it.

"This is my house," Therese whispered, remembering her father's words. "My rules."

She was twelve then, her stepsister was fourteen. It was too bad both their mothers had died. There was nothing Therese could do about that. Her own father was too busy, too successful to show any interest in her, much less in her mother. So when Therese realised that Aleksander Berndt cared enough to punish her, she decided he might just care enough to love her, to be proud of her, and to treat her like a daughter.

"And that's what he did, with a little help from me," she said, at the sound of the helicopter drilling another circle in the sky, sweeping the black sea with radar, night vision goggles, and *Mark 1* eyeballs. "Now it's time to make Daddy proud."

Therese tapped the screen and switched off the autopilot. The wheel twitched in her grasp, as the *Ophelia* trembled with the anticipation of being released, let off the hook, just as Therese hoped.

The Lynx thundered into another circular sweep. Therese squinted into the distance, caught the pinpricks of light which could have been the navigational lights of the *Ejnar Mikkelsen* or its big brother.

"It doesn't matter," she said. "This is my house. My rules."

Therese turned the *Ophelia* into the wind, stifling a grin as the bow bit into the first obsidian wave, crashing through the crest as Therese throttled up the side of the next wave, and the next, set after set, as she drove the *Ophelia* deeper into the Arctic waters of the Davis Strait.

"My house," she said. "My rules."

Chapter 18

Residents of Nuuk see the sun in winter. The days are short, but the sun makes an appearance, however brief. For Greenlanders living further north, in Inussuk, Uummannaq and in Qaanaaq – the most northerly village pretending to be a town – the sun does not shine for two to four months each winter. These northerly residents, Danes and Europeans among them especially, are easy to spot on winter flights from Kangerlussuaq to Copenhagen. When the Airbus 330-200 rises above the clouds, Nuuk residents tend to shield their eyes or turn away from the sun, while those from the north stare right at it, even though they shouldn't. Some, like Maratse, might acknowledge the sun with a mental dip of the head, a nod to a long-lost friend. It's been a while, they might say, and then turn away, fiddle with the foil-packed pretzels, or wonder if there is less leg room than the last time they flew on the Denmark flight. Others stare that bit longer, until the sun hurts their eyes, just as its absence hurts their soul. I'm struggling, they might say, won't you come back?

The sun comes back every year, rising at the same place, at the same time, unless the glacier has melted a little more since the previous year. Then the sun might return a day early, gone again if you missed it. The sun is visible in Uummannaq roughly fifteen minutes more each day after its first appearance in mid-January. In Qaanaaq the sun will shine thirty minutes longer than yesterday, from the day of its return around the eighteenth day of February. Once it has reached its summer height by the end of March, it won't set again before September. In Ittoqqortoormiit, on Maratse's east coast, the hunters, the fishermen, and their families share the same light and darkness as their west coast neighbours in Inussuk, only the mountains are different.

Maratse recognised a few of the passengers from his home town, and looked at them as he did the sun, just like intimate strangers.

"You're quiet," Petra said.

"I don't like planes."

"You don't like flying?" She took Maratse's packet of pretzels and opened them, splitting the packet down the middle as a hunter might gut a seal, exposing the innards.

"Just planes, the insides of them."

"You're just bored," Petra said, and ate a pretzel.

"*Iiji.*"

"Then why don't you read?"

"I need a new book." Maratse caught Petra's eye as she reached for the last pretzel. She lunged for it, giggling as the pretzel crumbled beneath her fingers.

"I like pretzels," she said.

"I can see that." Maratse wiped the crumbs into the foil packet, and pushed it inside his empty coffee cup, the wrapper crackled as it expanded within the circumference of the cup. Maratse wiped his hands, and said, "Tell me what the commissioner said."

"We're to meet with Hannah Mayer, a contact of his in the German Bundespolizei."

"I can't even say that."

"That's why the commissioner sent me. He said you were 'on your own dime', or something like that."

"Berndt's money," Maratse said, "he made a deposit into my account."

"Right." Petra waited as the flight attendant removed their empty cups. "Simonsen is going to visit Axel Stein. He'll probably send Danielsen."

"*Iiji.*"

"And the German captain, Katharina, will remain in custody until the deaths have been cleared up, all of them. As captain of the *Ophelia* she is responsible for her crew."

"And Nele?"

"I'm not sure. The German embassy has been putting pressure on the first minister, Nivi Winther, and she is pressurising the commissioner. He is stalling them by sending me to Berlin, but, as for Nele Schneider, I think she is being sent home, something about being traumatized and needing therapy from a German trauma psychologist, someone who speaks her own language."

"So, free to go?"

"I suppose so."

Maratse tapped his fingers on the tray table.

"You don't think she's innocent?"

"I don't think Dieter did it."

"And yet, he's the most likely suspect."

"Because he has no alibi."

"Because he was the only one not dead or drugged, and he attacked a police officer." Petra shrugged. "That's the circumstantial evidence. I didn't say he did it. But he has some interesting theories."

"The fake CVs?"

"And who knows what else. The CVs alone should be cause enough to dig deeper into who these people are. And what they were looking for."

"And Therese?"

"Apparently she slipped past the *Ejnar Mikkelsen*, but they are chasing her, and the *Knud Rasmussen* is heading for Cape Farewell to cut her off." Petra looked up at the clatter of the service trolley. "Once that part of the story breaks in the news, Greenland will gain a lot of exposure."

"And?"

"And that's exactly what Berndt wants." Petra leaned back as the flight attendant placed a tray on the table in front of her. She swapped Maratse's dessert for her salad.

"I like dessert," he said.

"But you don't eat enough vegetables." Petra slapped at the back of Maratse's hand as he tried to recover the plastic tub of chocolate mousse. He gave up, as Petra rearranged the items on her tray table, pushing the desserts further away from Maratse.

"You didn't finish," he said. "What does Berndt want?"

"He wants Uummannaq in focus so that he can apply emotional pressure to keep people away from Svartenhuk." Petra paused, and said, "Out of respect."

"For the dead?"

Petra nodded. She brushed a length of hair behind her ear, and prised the thick foil lid from the lasagne dish, stopping to blow on the tips of her fingers.

"You think he staged the murders?"

"No," Petra said, "but I think he intends to use them. It's convenient, otherwise he would have thought of something else."

"To keep people away from Svartenhuk?"

"To stop them digging around in the mountains." Petra folded the lid to one side, and opened the plastic bag of cutlery. "It's a shame you didn't read the journal."

"I can't read German."

"I know, but if you could, if there had been time, you might be the one who could prove what Wegener found in Svartenhuk."

Maratse thought about the snowmobile chase across the ice and Therese's long red hair as she pulled off her helmet to stare at him. He had been reluctant to get involved, and then he had been used.

"Next time, I won't get involved."

"With what?"

"An investigation. Of any kind."

"You'll just retire?"

"*Iiji,*" he said, "again."

"What if next time, the case is personal?"

"There won't be a next time." Maratse peeled back the lid of his lasagna.

"But if something happened to someone you care deeply for?" Petra turned her head, strands of jet black hair drifted over her cheek. She pulled them to one side with the tips of her nails, searching for Maratse's eyes with a deep brown gaze.

"I'll go fishing," he said, and plucked his dessert from Petra's tray. He waved his prize in front of her, and said, "You never know what I might catch."

"Fair enough, *Constable,*" Petra said, and leaned back in her seat. "But I don't think you can retire, not even if you tried."

Petra dozed after the meal, her head resting on Maratse's shoulder, her hand curled around his arm. He thought about what she said, about people he cared about – deeply. Yes, he realised, if anything happened to Petra, to Karl, Buuti, the people of Inussuk, even the temporary residents, he would not go fishing. He would hunt, instead, and he would find them, help them, solve the case, but not for money, he would do it because it was the right thing to do. He looked at Petra, and realised he would also do it out of love. He tugged a length of hair from the corner of Petra's mouth and brushed her cheek. She twitched and smiled at the light touch of his creased and calloused hands, squeezed his arm, and repositioned her head. She didn't wake before they landed in Copenhagen.

It was Petra who took over once they arrived in Denmark, leading Maratse through customs, vouching for him when she showed her police identity card, and collected her pistol.

"You're flying on to Berlin?" said the customs officer.

"Yes."

"Then you may as well leave that with me," he said, and nodded at the USP Compact pistol Petra was about to holster.

"I can do that?"

"It's the only thing you *can* do," he said. "It would be different if you were driving, or had official papers."

"We are meeting a German officer."

"Not good enough."

"Then I'll leave it with you."

Petra placed her pistol onto the desk and signed her weapon over to customs. She smiled at the officer, and then whisked Maratse through the crowds to the departure gate, shaking her head as he stopped and started while she weaved a line in and around the passengers.

"You're hopeless at this," she said, when she stopped to let him catch up for the fourth, maybe the fifth time. Petra laughed, as Maratse stopped to wait for another family, and then an older woman, and her daughter.

"There are fifty-eight people in Inussuk."

"And?"

"*Fifty-eight*, Piitalaat," Maratse said, as he hurried through a gap to stand next to Petra.

She took his hand. "Ready?"

"Holding hands?"

"It's that or we miss our flight," she said.

"I'm not ready for Berlin," he said.

"I can see that. But," Petra said, and tugged at Maratse's hand, "let's worry about that once we're on the flight."

Petra pulled Maratse through the crowd, all the way to the gate, letting go of his hand only when she thought he could keep up. Once they were boarded, buckled into their seats, and airborne, Petra stole the bag of peanuts from his tray.

"Airport tax," she said. The corners of her eyes twitched as she opened the peanuts, nibbling at them, one at a time, between smiles.

"Who are we meeting?" Maratse said, stirring sugar into his coffee.

"I told you earlier."

"I forgot."

"Hannah Mayer. I think the Commissioner worked with her in Nicaragua. Some kind of special task force. A bit like Polarpol."

"What's that?"

"Something I have been invited to be a part of."

"Like Europol?"

"Yes, I think so." Petra frowned. "The first meeting never really came to anything. There was this American, supposedly with the United States Geological Survey, although he admitted all of that was really only a cover."

"And he is with *Polarpol*?"

"I don't think so, but he had enough influence to end the meeting and pick my brains about the *Ophelia* case. This could come down as a simple case of murder for minerals."

"There's nothing simple about this case," Maratse said, and grabbed the peanuts from Petra's hand. The packet was empty.

Hannah Mayer called Petra's name as they walked through customs. She shook their hands, and then said, "Shall we speak English?"

"*Iiji*," Maratse said.

"That means, *yes*," Petra said, and tapped Maratse's arm. "Behave."

"You must be tired after the flight."

"Not yet," Petra said.

"All right then, that's good, because I want to take you to see Marlene Müller." Hannah gestured towards the exit, pulling her car keys from her pocket as she began to walk. "I spoke to her this morning. She is quite shaken, but very keen to meet you both, especially you, David. She heard that you pulled her husband out of a car that was sinking through the ice. Is that right?"

"I helped," Maratse said.

"It's true," Petra said, "but there are also lots of questions, still unanswered, regarding Dieter's whereabouts, and his involvement in the murders."

Hannah paused at the door to pull up the collar of her jacket. Maratse shivered as they stepped out of the airport and into the damp cold of Berlin. Hannah smiled at him as she held the door.

"The murders of the *Ophelia* crew? Yes, I understand," Hannah said, as they approached a black Mercedes Benz. "Lars briefed me over the phone." She clicked the fob on her keyring. "This is us."

Maratse buckled up as Hannah pulled out of her parking spot and accelerated into the late-afternoon Berlin traffic. She switched on the GPS unit, clicked on a preset button, and used the radio mounted to the dash to check-in with her department as the map of their route loaded onto the screen. Maratse watched their progress from the backseat.

"Albertstraße, the street where Marlene lives, is not the nicest of areas, but it's not a slum. We'll be there shortly." She glanced in the rear-view mirror. "Shall I turn up the heat?"

"Please," Maratse said.

Hannah smiled. "I thought it was cold in Greenland?"

"Not like this."

"It's the damp," Petra said. "Although David thinks Nuuk is cold too."

"It is," Maratse said. He zipped his jacket and stuffed his hands in his pockets.

"Is that a police jacket?" Hannah said. "It looks like Petra's."

"*Iiji.*"

"You used to be a policeman?"

"David is retired," Petra said. She turned in her seat to catch his eye, continuing when he nodded. "He was the first on the scene. The first to find the yacht."

"And you were also with Dieter in the car?"

"Yes," Petra said. "He was involved in the search for Dieter Müller."

"Is that what they call retirement in Greenland?" Hannah caught Maratse's eye in the mirror.

"I'm working on it."

Petra laughed. "He really is."

"Okay," Hannah said, as she slowed for traffic. "We're nearly there. Tell me what we're looking for."

"Dieter received some information in the mail, CVs to be specific, for the crew of the *Ophelia*. He left the originals at his apartment, together with his notes, but scanned the documents onto a thumb drive."

"Which was stolen?"

"So he says."

"And you want the originals?"

"No, we want to see if he has a copy on his computer. We understand the originals were taken, together with his notes, by a man supposedly working for Aleksander Berndt."

Hannah nodded as she turned onto Albertstraße and looked for a place to park.

"You might be too late. When I called Marlene she told me that when the man took Dieter's notes he took the computer as well. She gave him everything, so we can't even accuse Berndt of stealing. Apparently, the man told her he needed access to everything to be able to help Dieter. Dieter's face has been all over the newspapers, Berndt's included." Hannah paused to park the car. She turned off the engine, and said, "Marlene is pretty keyed-up. I think her doctor wanted to prescribe Valium, but she refused. She just wants Dieter home. She is going to ask you when that might happen."

Hannah opened the door and waited on the street for Petra and Maratse to join her. She pointed at the door on the other side of the street; it was tagged with graffiti, as were the shutters protecting the windows of the local shops. Hannah's car was the newest and brightest car in a long line of rusting European cars, sporting bruised panels and bald tyres. She led them to the door and stopped, one finger extended to push the button to Marlene's apartment.

"What is it?" Petra asked.

Hannah nodded in the direction of a black Sprinter van, perhaps only a year older than her Mercedes. "It's probably nothing." She pushed the button, and opened the door as Marlene buzzed them into the building.

Chapter 19

Heat leaked out of the windows of Marlene Müller's apartment, but it was still the first time Maratse had felt warm since arriving in Germany. She showed them to the living room, excused the mess and disappeared into the tiny kitchen to make tea. Maratse understood little of what was said in the beginning, but, as Petra started to translate, he noticed that Marlene would pause after everything she said. That and the way she looked at him suggested it was important for her that he could follow the conversation. Maratse sipped his tea, and nodded for her to continue.

"She's worried, naturally," Petra whispered. "And the guy Berndt sent to pick up the notes and the computer – she doesn't trust him."

"She has no reason to," Hannah said, "not after Berndt released a statement to the press with a detailed description of Dieter's battle with depression."

"He made him a *Sündenbock*," Marlene said.

"A scapegoat," Petra said.

"*Ja, das ist korrekt.*"

Tea from Marlene's mug splashed onto the table as she put it down. She hadn't touched it, Maratse noticed. He watched her get up and walk to the bedroom, when she returned she had a plastic shopping bag in her hand. She placed it on the table. Hannah leaned over and opened it.

"An external hard drive," she said, and folded the sides of the bag to reveal a small hard drive with a USB cable attached.

"A backup," Petra said, once Marlene had finished speaking. Petra asked something in German, Marlene answered, and Maratse waited for Petra to confirm that everything was on the hard drive, including the scans of the documents he received in the mail. "We can use this," Petra said.

"*Iiji.*"

"When will Dieter come home?"

"That's difficult, Marlene," Hannah said. "We're working on it. One, he has to be fit to travel, and two, he has to be allowed to travel." She paused as Petra translated for Maratse. "There are still lots of unanswered questions."

Maratse placed his mug on the table and leaned back in the sofa. He found a tear in the cushions and resisted the urge to pick at it. The condition of the sofa, the tired wallpaper on the walls, and the faint smell of damp surprised him. He had seen worse conditions in Greenland, but, in comparison, there was not a great deal of difference. He allowed himself to feel some of Marlene's despair, shelving his professional objectiveness for a moment. He was, after all, retired. A change in tempo, and Petra's light tap on his knee suggested that they were leaving. Maratse stood up and thanked Marlene for the tea.

"You're welcome," she said, her accent abrasive, like the tears stinging her cheeks.

Maratse waited for Petra to pick up the plastic bag, and then followed Hannah out of the apartment and down the stairs. He heard the squeal of tyres as Hannah opened the door to the street.

The first pop of bullets surprised them, the impact

louder than the act of firing. Maratse wondered for a second if the shooter was using a silencer screwed onto the barrel of his weapon, but then Petra pulled him down the steps and Hannah returned fire, loosing two rounds, and then a third into the side of a dark Sprinter van, the same one she had spotted earlier.

The side door rumbled open to reveal a man holding onto a length of rope looped into the roof with one hand, and a Heckler & Koch MP5 with the other. Hannah shot him twice in the chest as he pulled the trigger. The submachine gun spit an arc of bullets in a burst that chipped stone from the steps, chunks of masonry from the walls, and shattered the window of the downstairs apartment. Maratse shoved Petra over a low wall and into a sunken garden, a metre below street level. He stumbled down the steps as Petra disappeared from view and a second man leaped out of the van. The driver emptied the magazine of his Beretta at Hannah, forcing her behind two parked cars as Maratse tumbled onto the pavement.

"David," Petra shouted, as the passenger of the van hit Maratse on the back of the head and dragged him inside. The driver accelerated down the street and the last man dived inside the van. Hannah fired at the retreating vehicle as the man pulled the dead shooter inside and slammed the door shut.

Maratse pressed his hand against the back of his head, his hair matted and tacky beneath his fingers. He squinted in the gloom of the van, saw his assailant fumble the MP5 from the dead man's grip, change magazines, and turn to point the submachine gun at Maratse. He held up his hands, slipped to one side as the van squealed around a corner, and then settled onto his knees. The man holding the MP5 nodded, and banged on the tiny window between the cargo area and the cab, shouting something that made the driver slow down.

"Don't do anything stupid," the man said in English.

"Okay," Maratse said.

They stared at each other for another ten minutes before the driver slowed to a stop, and the man with the gun opened the door. He snapped his fingers for Maratse to follow him. Once out of the van, Maratse blinked in the harsh glare of the streetlights, as they walked past large rubbish bins, stacks of flat pizza boxes, and crates of empty bottles. The man reached out and grabbed Maratse by the arm, pulling him through an open door and into a kitchen as the driver closed the van and drove away.

The kitchen was bright compared to the mood lighting of the restaurant. He bumped into the back of a chair as the man led him around the empty tables. Maratse glanced at the windows, but could see nothing of the street, the blinds were drawn. His head hurt when he turned at the sound of a chair being dragged out from beneath a table. The man pushed Maratse into it, tugged thin plastic strips from his pocket and tied Maratse's wrists, lower arms, and ankles to the chair legs and arms. He looped another strip through Maratse's belt, and tied him to the back of the chair. Maratse watched as the man checked the ties, pulled the sling of the MP5 over his head, and slid the weapon onto the red-and-white-checked tablecloth of a table against the wall. He pulled a second weapon, a pistol, from his pocket and tucked it into the waistband at the front of his jeans. The man rested against the table in front of Maratse and lit a cigarette.

Maratse felt his body begin to charge itself in

anticipation of the next stage in what he felt was an all too familiar situation. If he closed his eyes he would see the Chinese man, metal paddles in hand, standing in front of him in the cabin of a remote mining camp, deep in the fjord north of Nuuk. He might even hear him complain at the unreliable generator, spluttering to keep up with the demands of torture. But Maratse would not close his eyes. Even so, the American voice, when he heard it, surprised him.

"Constable David Maratse," the American said, as he walked around Maratse and stood next to the man with the gun. "Retired."

"*Iiji.*"

"You look resigned to that chair, and your record – the little that is available – suggests that if I told you my name, you might fear the worst, knowing that I would have to make sure you couldn't repeat it."

Maratse dug deep, and was surprised for a second time by his response. "You could give me a false name."

"And tell you it was false? To what end?"

"To give me hope."

The American snorted, pulled the gun from the other man's waistband, and said, "Stefan, get us a drink." He tapped the barrel of the Beretta against the surface of the table and studied Maratse. "You're funny, Constable. Not as pretty as your friend, but funny."

"My friend?"

"Sergeant Jensen," said the American. "Who should be here," he said, with a look at Stefan as he returned with a bottle of whisky and shot glasses gripped between his fingers. "Three glasses, Stefan? You really think you have cause for celebration?"

Stefan put the glasses on the table. He shrugged

as he uncorked the whisky. "They had a German cop with them. She returned fire."

"Of course she did." The American took a glass of whisky from Stefan's hand. "That's what she's trained to do."

"All the same," Stefan said, and downed a shot of whisky, "that's why he's alone."

"All right," the American said. He took a slug of whisky and then slapped the Beretta into Stefan's palm. "I guess we just have to do this the hard way." He pointed at the third glass of whisky. "That's for you, Constable, when we're done. Just to keep you amiable."

The American pulled a mobile from his pocket and dragged the table so that Maratse's knees were beneath the surface. He placed the mobile in the middle. Stefan took off his jacket and rolled up his sleeves. Maratse stared at the snake tattoos twisting from the man's wrists to his elbow. Stefan winked at him.

"In German, if you please," the American said, and pointed at the mobile. Stefan picked it up and dialled a number, as the American laid a heavy hand on Maratse's shoulder. "You probably know how this works. Your friend has something I want, and I have you."

"You want the hard drive?"

"Amongst other things." He smiled, and raised a hand for Stefan to wait a second. "Can I be candid with you, Constable?"

Maratse nodded.

"I'm surprised to say this, but I find our friend incredibly attractive. You agree, of course?"

Maratse said nothing, but the bitter taste in his mouth must have tightened the skin around his eyes, because the American laughed, and slapped him on the shoulder.

"You see," he said, "Already we have something in common. A love of dark, attractive women." He spun his finger and Stefan pressed the dial button and placed the mobile on the table.

When a female voice answered, Stefan said, "Hannah Mayer?"

"Ja?"

Stefan spoke in German as he looked at Maratse, but Hannah answered in English.

"I need proof that you have David Maratse, that he is well."

The American slapped the back of Maratse's head, and said, "You're on."

"Hannah, this is Maratse."

"Are you all right?"

"I'm tied up in…"

A second blow from the American fused the words behind Maratse's bloody lips. The chair tipped to one side, and the American helped it crash to the floor with a toe beneath one leg as Stefan grabbed the phone from the table.

"I'm going to text you with an address. Bring the hard drive in one hour," Stefan said. "Send the Eskimo." He swiped the screen to end the call.

"One hour?" the American said. "That's cutting it a little fine."

Stefan shrugged. "It's up to your asset now."

"Sure."

The American knelt down beside Maratse. He held out his hand, and Stefan pressed the glass of whisky into it. The American poured the whisky onto Maratse's face, dribbling it into his eyes. Maratse blinked and tried to turn away.

"This is a waste," the American said, and gripped Maratse by the hair. "But I heard Greenlanders like their drink."

"Some Greenlanders," Maratse said, and licked whisky and blood from his lips.

"Only some?" The American tossed the glass at Stefan, and said, "Help me get him up."

The plastic straps dug into Maratse's skin as the two men pulled the chair onto its legs. He let his head roll back and then forwards, wiping the blood from his chin on the collar of his jacket.

"Your friend," the American said, "thinks my name is Johnson, so that's the name you can use. How about that, Constable?"

"It's a false name?"

"It's one of many. Why?"

Maratse spat a clot of blood from his mouth, and said, "Just wondering if I'm going to live."

Johnson folded his arms and looked at Maratse. "You're a curious one," he said. "This really isn't your first time, is it?"

"This is better than my first time."

"Ha," Johnson said, and pulled up a chair beside Maratse. He sat down, and said, "Do tell."

"There's nothing to tell."

"Because it's confidential?" Johnson gestured for Stefan to give him the bottle of whisky. "But you're among friends, Constable." He uncorked the whisky and mashed the glass lip of the bottle into Maratse's mouth. "Now," he said, and tipped the bottle, "either your teeth rotted out or were pulled out, which is it?"

Maratse spluttered on the whisky. He turned his head, but Stefan walked behind him, clamped bony hands around his ears and jaw, and tipped his head backwards. Maratse squinted in the light above, coughed and choked on the whisky.

"Come on, Constable. This isn't even about you. Just give us a few details from your life, and explain to me why that pretty young Petra finds you so attractive – a retired constable with bad teeth and a wispy beard. Hell, Stefan," he said, "I might even be in with a chance here. I mean I'm only ten years or so older than the constable, and he's practically twice her age." He laughed, and then removed the bottle as Maratse spluttered to talk. "What's that?"

"Thirteen."

"Your lucky number?" Johnson winked at Stefan.

"Thirteen years older."

"Ah," Johnson said, "I get it. You've done the math. And you know what that means don't you, Stefan?"

"What does it mean?"

Johnson lifted the bottle to the light, sloshing the contents in front of Maratse's eyes; there was half a bottle left.

"It means the constable here is interested. He might even shave that ridiculous beard if the young Petra with those dark almond eyes, chocolate skin, and silky black hair, popped the question, or, you know, just grabbed him one night. I mean, if that's not worth a drink, I don't know what is."

Johnson pressed the bottle to Maratse's lips as Stefan held his head. Maratse tried to concentrate, to listen to the tiny voice reassuring him that most of the whisky was dribbling down his chin, onto his clothes, but the whisky burned, prevented him from breathing, and Maratse realised once again what he already knew to be true, torture wasn't about information, it was never about information, it was all about power. The American knew that, and Maratse had the idea that this wasn't his first time either.

Maratse coughed, ratcheting air into his body as Stefan let go of his head, and he spluttered whisky from his lungs. Johnson tossed the bottle onto the floor and it rolled beneath a table.

"Waste of a good bourbon," he said, and gripped Maratse's chin between thick fingers. "What do you think, Constable? Had enough?"

Chapter 20

Petra slammed her palm against the interior panel as the driver swung the heavy assault vehicle around the roundabout and accelerated away from the *Siegessaule*. Hannah tugged at the straps on Petra's vest while a member of the German GSG 9 group stuffed ceramic plates into the back of the vest. He lifted a ballistic helmet from the seat and tried to press it onto Petra's head.

"If I wear that, they will think I'm one of you," she said, and waved him away.

"You might get shot," he said.

"I *will* get shot if I'm wearing that thing."

Hannah nodded for the man to step away and guided Petra into a spare seat.

Petra took a breath of adrenalin-stoked air, glanced at the men and women of the Bundespolizei's counter terrorism unit, and forced a smile for Hannah. "I'm okay," she said.

"I know." Hannah smiled. "Greenlanders are tough, eh?"

"I wouldn't know," Petra said. "I guess so."

"This one is," Hannah said. She slapped Petra on the thigh and dug into a satchel on the seat beside her. Hannah handed Petra a thin sheath of papers. "The CVs," she said. "We printed them off the hard drive."

Petra flicked through the documents, as Hannah sat down beside her.

"Do you know what you are looking for?"

"Not yet."

Petra lurched into the shoulder of the policeman checking his gear beside her. He smiled and said something about a rookie driver. Petra nodded, braced herself for another turn, and then looked up when Hannah called her name.

"Call for you," she said, pressing her phone into Petra's hand. "It's Lars."

"Commissioner," Petra said, as she held the phone to her ear.

"This is the official *talk*, Sergeant."

"Yes, sir."

"I need to hear you say you volunteered for this."

"I did."

"Say it."

"I volunteered, sir."

"All right. Now I need to know why?"

"They have Maratse." She waited as the commissioner sighed.

"I understand," he said. "What I don't understand, is what this has to do with the case? I sent you to Germany to find answers, not stir up a storm. You've been gone less than twenty-four hours. What's going on?"

"They want the hard drive. I think they are trying to erase all the evidence."

"What evidence?"

"The real identities of the *Ophelia* crew. Once we know who they really are, we'll be able to confirm what they were really doing in Svartenhuk, and why people had to die for it."

"Who's they?"

"I don't know, but we are heading to the offices of the Berndt Media Group. I think we can assume that he is involved."

"He hasn't been picked up by the police?"

"They are looking for him, Sir." Petra looked at Hannah. She nodded. "What about Berndt's daughter?" Petra bounced off the shoulder of the man on her left as they drove over a set of asphalt speed bumps.

"Now that's a topic I haven't talked about at all today."

"Sir?"

"I think the first minister, the German ambassador, and the Danish foreign minister have my number on speed dial, but then I have the general major for Arctic Command's number, and he is just as tired of me as I am of them."

"Where is Therese?"

"She is approaching Cape Farewell with full sails. The commander can't decide if she is talented or suicidal. He suspects both. She's riding with the storm, and the size of the waves is making it impossible for the crew from either the *Ejnar Mikkelsen* or the *Knud Rasmussen* to board her. The helicopters are grounded."

"So she's getting away?"

"She'll either get away or die trying, that seems to be the general opinion. That's some journal you found."

"Yes, sir."

"Personally, I don't know how much it has to do with the journal. The way she sails, well, I believe the devil drives." The commissioner paused to take an incoming call, when he came back, he asked to speak to Hannah. Petra handed her the phone and tucked the documents into her vest.

"Yes," Hannah said. "I'll look after her." Hannah smiled. "Yes. I agree."

Petra frowned as Hannah slipped her phone into her pocket.

"What was that last bit about?"

"He's very fond of you, thinks you are a very competent police officer. I agreed."

"Thank you."

"Don't thank me, Sergeant," Hannah said, as the driver slowed and turned off the siren. "I'm about to send you into the lion's den."

"We don't know that."

"Oh, I think we do." The vehicle stopped and Hannah waited for the team to get out before standing up. "It's not every day we have a shoot out on the streets of Berlin. Make no mistake; we don't know what's inside that building, which is why I requested GSG 9, and not just the regular police. These guys are the best."

"That sounded like a pep talk," Petra said, as she followed Hannah out of the vehicle and onto the street.

"It was." Hannah led Petra to an officer standing beside the second van. Petra could only see his eyes. His height, his gear, and the weapon slung across his chest reminded her of Gaba. When she looked at the team members, she realised they all did.

"Great," she whispered, "I'm channelling my ex-boyfriend."

"What's that?" Hannah asked.

"Nothing. I'm ready."

"Okay." Hannah introduced Petra to the GSG 9 leader and took a step back.

"You're Sergeant Jensen?"

"Yes."

"Right, here's what you need to know."

Petra listened as the leader of the counter

terrorism team described the layout of the building, the location of the office on the second floor, and a detailed description of the lobby and reception, the position of the elevators, and the stairwells.

Petra nodded when he asked if she understood.

"Good," he said. "Do you have the package?"

Petra tapped the front pocket of her vest.

"And the wire? Your mic?" He turned to the officer on his right. The man tapped his headphones and gave him the thumbs-up. "Okay." He took a step back. "This is the back-brief. Tell me what the plan is."

Petra glanced at Hannah. "I go inside, take the elevator to the second floor, meet with the contact, ask for the location of Constable David Maratse, and give them the hard drive. No negotiations. I won't try to bargain. I'll repeat the address," she said, and pressed her fingers to the microphone hidden beneath her collar, "then I leave the hard drive on the floor, and go back to the elevator."

"Good," the man said. He stepped behind Petra, held her by the shoulders and turned her to look at the position of the sniper teams in the opposite buildings. He tilted her head to see the teams scrambling into position on the roof, and then dipped her head to see the GSG 9 men taking position behind cars, and ballistic shields. "We are deliberately overt," he said, and let go of Petra. "We want the kidnappers to see us *before* you go in. If they've done this before, they will give you the address once they are clear of the building, but then we've got the GPS tracker hidden inside the casing of the hard drive. Hopefully, the sight of so many heavily armed, steely-eyed professional marksmen will put them off doing anything stupid." The man tugged at the balaclava hiding his mouth. "I'm smiling, Sergeant."

"Okay."

"We've got your back."

"I know."

"Now, will you put on a helmet?"

"No," she said, and took a breath. "I'm ready."

Hannah thanked the GSG 9 leader, curled her arm around Petra's, and guided her to a gap in the police cordon, nodding at the officers as they passed. She stopped three metres beyond the police line.

"He didn't tell you about the teams already inside the building."

"Inside?"

"In the basement, working their way up."

"They only had an hour."

Hannah shrugged, and said, "They're good. They've got your back, now it's up to you to go in there and make the exchange."

Petra looked up at the large glass windows. The lights were dimmed.

"Do you think he's in there?"

"David? No, I don't think so."

"Neither do I."

"The truth is, we have no idea what to expect. You probably won't even recognise the person inside. Hell, it could even be a drone, remotely piloted from one of these buildings," she said, and waved a finger at the offices overlooking the Berndt Media Group building. "Maybe there's a pouch on the drone, and..."

"Hannah," Petra said.

"Yes, sorry," she said. "I was getting carried away. But, hey, now you have plenty to think about."

"I liked the other pep talk better," Petra said, and made a sound that could almost have been interpreted as a laugh. She gripped Hannah's hand for a second, nodded once, and let go. Petra walked across the street, stepped up onto the pavement, and continued walking to the door.

As soon as she entered the elevator, Petra realised Hannah had been wrong about the contact person being a stranger; she recognised Nele Schneider the moment the young German woman pressed the barrel of a gun into her cheek.

"Going up?" Nele asked, as she pressed the button for the sixth floor, and then ripped Petra's microphone from her throat. She tossed it into the lobby as the elevator doors hushed to a close.

Nele pushed Petra against the wall of the elevator, shifted the barrel of the gun to Petra's forehead, and then opened the Velcro pouch at the front of her vest. She tucked the hard drive into the cargo pocket of her trousers and took a step back.

"This is where it gets complicated," she said.

"It doesn't have to, Nele."

"Nele? That's right, that's my name." She shrugged. "Sometimes I forget. It's not easy playing the victim all the time. It's far more fun to get physical, if you know what I mean?"

"I'm not sure I do." Petra worked on her breathing, felt her chest press against the inside of the vest, wondered if it would help to loosen the straps, and then decided that it wouldn't.

Not one bit.

Nele glanced at the elevator's progress, grabbed Petra by the hair, and pressed the gun to the side of her head. When the elevator doors opened, Nele kicked Petra's legs, dropping the sergeant to her knees, and then ducked behind her. She made Petra shuffle into the corridor, turning her like a shield with a twist of her hair, first to the left, then right. Satisfied,

Nele told Petra to get up, and then shoved her forwards, through the open office, and into a more luxurious workspace with a door, and a large side window facing the street. The rear wall of the office separated the Berndt building from the adjoining offices of an insurance company. Nele flicked off the lights and pushed Petra into the corner.

"Snipers," she said. "I know their game."

"Who are you?" Petra asked, as Nele relaxed her grip on her hair.

"That's not important."

"Where's Maratse?"

Nele laughed, and said, "That's even less important."

"You have what you want. You can at least tell me where he is."

"He's safe," Nele said, "for the moment."

Petra crumpled to her knees as Nele let go. She watched as the young German woman opened a black backpack tucked beneath a desk. She pulled out a remote with two large safety switches. Nele grinned and mouthed the word *boom* at Petra.

So this is how it feels, Petra thought, as she imagined Maratse being tortured by the Chinese man. This is how it feels when someone holds your life in their hands, and has every intention of ending it. Total control, total power.

"You're thinking too much," Nele said. "Stop it. It bothers me."

"Why?"

"Because I'm working on getting out of here. Your friends are good," she said, with a nod to the street. "I should know, I trained with them once or twice."

"You're a soldier?"

Nele laughed. "I might have been, if he hadn't found me."

"Who?"

"You'll see," she said, with a nod to the whiteboard covering the adjoining wall. Petra watched as Nele crawled to the wall, tugged a set of wires from behind the whiteboard, and attached them to the remote in her hand. She crawled back to Petra, and then toppled a desk in front of them.

"You're going to blow us up?"

"I'm going to blow *that* up," she said, and pointed at the wall. "That's our way out."

"You're taking me with you?"

"Sure," Nele said, "I need insurance." She furrowed her brow and said, "Of course, premiums are high, and I can't promise to keep up the payments. Do you understand?"

"You'll shoot me."

"Shoot you? Hell no, Eskimo, I'll *kill* you."

Petra ignored the pressure in her bladder, and took a chance. "Like you killed the crew of the *Ophelia*?" Nele whipped her head around and stared at Petra. "You stabbed them to death, didn't you?"

"You can't prove that."

"I don't need to, if you tell me." It was Petra's turn to shrug. "You're going to kill me, you said so."

"I did," Nele frowned. "But why do I get the feeling you are playing me?"

"Because I want you to save Maratse. I don't care about me."

"The old guy with the funny beard?"

"Yes," Petra said. She felt the corners of her mouth twitch, and she amazed herself with a smile. "He means a lot to me."

"There's a shortage of men in Greenland?"

"Not exactly."

"Then why?"

"You wouldn't understand. I love him."

Nele stared at her, and then turned the remote in her hand. Petra continued.

"You didn't love Henrik."

"What?"

"You wouldn't have stabbed him if you did."

"Henrik had to go."

"Because he found out about Arbroath Mining?" Petra waited as Nele shuffled closer. When Nele was close enough that Petra could smell the sweat beneath her shirt, she said, "But you didn't need to kill Antje, unless…"

"Unless what?" Nele said, her top lip twisted, a cruel slant.

"You did love Henrik. That's it, isn't it?"

"I was told someone had to die. That was my role on the expedition. Not ski guide or mountaineer. That's what I was hired for, but my job was to kill. To make a mess."

"Who hired you? Berndt?"

"You won't get that from me."

"But Antje?"

"Henrik tried to stop me. He woke up too soon." Nele shook her head. "I only put half the drug in my drink. I think he took that one. I had to put more in his ear, couldn't cope with his screams."

Petra heard something click outside the door. She kept talking.

"What about Dieter?"

"Hah, fall guy, the patsy. Idiot." Nele laughed. "He made it easy. Wouldn't go back to the yacht. Something about not trusting himself around the captain."

"So you left him on the mountain?"

"Hardly. We were on the path to that cabin the Greenlanders like to keep so secret, like it's a shrine. He said he knew where it was. All I had to do was push him to disobey orders, turn him against Henrik."

"So you could kill them and pin the murder on Dieter?"

"It was a good plan. Guilty lover, confused with exposure. He was supposed to die on the mountain."

"But he didn't."

"No," Nele said, as she clicked the remote.

The blast from the shape charge behind the whiteboard filled the room with a cloud of grey plaster, as the whiteboard shattered the window opposite the wall, and revealed a hole into the adjoining office. Nele scrambled over the desk, and disappeared through the cloud. Petra scrabbled on the floor, shuffling bits of debris through her fingers as she picked herself up, and staggered after Nele.

The second explosion was louder and brighter than the first, but without the physical shock of the blast. Petra tumbled to her knees as the GSG 9 team crashed through the office, green lasers lancing through the plaster cloud as they moved through over the rubble, the stocks of their submachine guns pressed to their shoulders, the barrels and lasers sweeping left and right in sync with their eyes.

One man knelt beside Petra as the rest of the team moved forwards. He wiped dust from her eyes with rough brushes of his thumb, turned her head to check her ears for blood, to see if her eardrums had been perforated in the explosion, and told her to stay put. He pressed his fingers to the microphone around his throat and then gagged as Nele crawled out from beneath a desk, and slid a knife into the base of the man's skull. He toppled forwards on top of Petra, as Nele tugged the pistol from her waistband and aimed it at the rearguard of the GSG 9 team. She loosed off two shots before she was shot in the back, by team two moving in from the rear.

Nele slumped to her knees, and took another two bullets in her back before collapsing at Petra's feet. Petra crawled free of the GSG 9 man pinning her to the ground, and twisted Nele onto her back.

"Where is Maratse?" she shouted, as Nele started to gag on the blood in her mouth. Nele's head lolled back to her neck, and Petra caught it. "Where is he?"

"You already know," Nele said, as her body slumped to the ground.

Two men from the GSG 9 team worked on the body of their fallen team member, as the other men cleared the room. The first team returned, declared the area clear, and then clumped around the men working on the man with Nele's knife in his head.

Petra searched Nele's pockets, and tucked the hard drive into her vest before one of the team pulled her to her feet. He took her through the hole in the wall, and found a chair for her in the middle of the open office.

"Stay here," he said, "Mayer is on her way up."

Petra waited for him to hurry back to the medics, and then slipped out of the office. She took the stairs, stumbling all the way to the ground floor. Petra pushed through the fire door, and staggered down the street, holding her ears as the fire alarm drilled into her head.

She hailed a taxi, cursed it as the driver took one look at her, and drove on. The same happened with the second, but the third taxi stopped. Petra opened the passenger door, and pulled the documents from inside her vest.

"Where to?"

Petra laid the documents on her bloody lap. She found three with the same address in the references section, whispered a quick thanks to such sloppy attention to detail, and told the driver where to go.

Chapter 21

The plastic strip securing Maratse's ankle to the chair leg snapped just before midnight. His foot twitched and knocked one of the empty bottles of whisky. It rolled under the table and rattled against another, the sound of glass knocking against glass woke him, and he tried hard to open his eyes. Johnson pressed two fingers under Maratse's chin and lifted it, prising one eye open with the fingers of his other hand.

"To be fair," Johnson said, "I thought Greenlanders had a weakness for alcohol, something in their genes that means they can't handle their drink." He let go of Maratse's chin, sucking air through his teeth with a whooshing sound as Maratse's head snapped to his chest. "But this one did okay. Although he's gonna have a hell of a hangover in the morning." Johnson turned to Stefan, and said, "She should have been here by now. She should have called."

Stefan waved the iPhone. "Nothing. Not even a text."

"All right," Johnson said. "Phase two. Go and get Berndt." He looked at his watch. "If we can get this sorted before office hours tomorrow, I can fly back to the States, be home with the wife for Thanksgiving."

Stefan stopped at the door. "You want me to bring anything to eat?"

"You do know we are in a restaurant?"

Stefan shrugged. "I don't like Italian."

"Whatever." Johnson waved his hand. "Just bring me Berndt, and soon."

Johnson waited until Stefan had left, and then picked up the empty whisky bottles, lining them up on the table in front of Maratse, until he had a row of three. He picked up a spoon and tapped the side of one of the bottles until Maratse lifted his head and squinted at him.

"There you are, Constable. I'm bored. Entertain me."

Maratse had the vague sensation of drool dribbling from the corner of his mouth. Another sensation, a pressure in his bladder, made him realise he needed to piss, but he couldn't recall if he had already, or just needed to. He tried to focus on Johnson as he placed a fourth bottle of whisky on the table.

"Don't worry," he said, "you spilled most of that one."

"Why?" Maratse said, the word longer and more complicated than he remembered.

"We don't always need a reason, do we? Why do anything?" Johnson dragged a chair across the floor, placed it beside Maratse, and sat down. "We're driven," he said, and patted Maratse's arm. "Some are more driven than others, I'll grant you that, but we are each, in our own way driven to do things. If you ask me, greed drives most people. A want for more. I see it every day. They might *want* different things such as power, a new car, a bigger house, but greed drives them. I'll admit to being a little power hungry at times, but I wouldn't say that drives me, not completely." He stopped, leaned closer to Maratse, encouraging him with small, slow waves of his hand. "You can do it. That's it."

"What then?" Maratse said.

"Well it's not lust, not all the time, but sex is certainly something that drives me. I mean, you must be having sex up there in Greenland, eh? Not much else to do in that crab-fart of a settlement in the winter. No," Johnson said, "I think I'm driven more out of curiosity. For example," he said, and leaned forwards, "take this particular job, chasing a forgotten journal half-way around the world, just to find out if an area is viable for mining, you know? I found that curious. My curiosity was aroused."

Johnson clicked his fingers in front of Maratse's face, sighed, pushed back his chair, and walked into the kitchen. When he came back, he emptied a jug of cold water over Maratse's head.

"I find that stimulating conversations work best when both parties are awake, Constable. Now," he said, as Maratse spluttered at the water dribbling over his lips, "as I was saying." Johnson put the jug on the table. "This job was about solving a problem. As you know, the Greenland government, in their wisdom, put a stop to geological surveys in areas within one hundred kilometres of towns, villages, and settlements. They were a bit more accommodating with what you call 'living places' with one or two inhabitants too stubborn to die, but Svartenhuk was out of bounds. Unless – and this is where I pride myself on being more than a little ingenious – a survey had already been carried out, prior to the new law in 2013."

"Wegener," Maratse said.

"Exactly. Well done, Constable, I'm so pleased you are keeping up."

"My pleasure." Maratse moved his lips into what he thought was a smile.

"Ah, yes," Johnson said. "One thing at a time, I think." He tapped the table, and said, "I heard a rumour that an old acquaintance was speculating in a Scottish mining company. Arbroath Mining is the name. My friend knows nothing about mining, but he does know the energy business. Nuclear energy to be precise. Tell me, Constable, have you heard of thorium? No?" Johnson reached over to the next table and tugged a napkin from beneath the cutlery and wiped Maratse's chin. He tossed the napkin into Maratse's lap. "Thorium is a radioactive mineral, and can be used to produce nuclear energy, more or less on a par with uranium. My friend discovered two things of interest concerning Arbroath Mining Company." Johnson held up a finger. "One, they were struggling. And two." Another finger. "When Arbroath bought the rights to the old marble mine in Uummannaq, they also bought the rights that included the mountains of Svartenhuk. Now, Arbroath might be struggling, but they had a solid business plan – invest everything in proving the viability of their concern, and then get bought out by a bigger company. Bigger companies tend to keep an eye on the likes of Arbroath, but it is a risky strategy, as they are just as likely to be forgotten."

"Not by you."

"Again, Constable, I must praise you for keeping track. Remarkable, really," Johnson said, with a nod to the row of empty bottles on the table. "My curiosity was peaked. I looked into Arbroath, Greenland, even Wegener, and I discovered a riddle, that might, if it were solved, prove very profitable to the people I represent." Johnson laughed. "Is that a look of surprise? I can't tell, but let's assume that it is. I'm not personally capable of fronting this operation, although

I'm flattered you might think so. No, I'm just good at pointing the right people in the right direction, at the right time, and then adding a few elements of my own to spice things up."

"Like Nele Schneider?" Petra said, as she opened the door to the kitchen. "I let myself in," she said, and raised the pistol in her hand.

"Sergeant Jensen," Johnson said, and clapped. "Good girl. I can see why they picked you for the task force." He gestured at Maratse. "Your friend and I were having a chat over a few drinks, although the constable did most of the drinking. He's got quite a thirst."

"Are you all right, David?"

"*Iiji.*"

Petra pointed the gun at Johnson, and said, "Untie him."

"What happens if I say no?"

Petra pulled the trigger and clipped Johnson's shoulder with a bullet from Nele's gun. The American swore, checked his shoulder, and lifted his hand to show Petra a stripe of blood across his fingers. "That, Sergeant, was not smart."

"Untie him."

"Fine." Johnson pulled a buck knife from his boot, opened the blade, and locked it in place, cutting the ties, one by one. "I must say, you look a little rough, Sergeant. How is Nele?"

"Dead," Petra said, and waved the gun. "Keep going."

"That's unfortunate. She was quite useful."

"She said she was ordered to make a mess, something newsworthy. Did you tell her to do that?"

"Anything to do with the news is Berndt's business, literally. I told her to kill Henrik Baumann because he was an activist. Greenpeace, or some other organisation with more balls than money. I thought he might destroy the journal before we had made use of it." Johnson cut the ties around Maratse's hands. "There's another one through his belt," he said, and offered the knife to Petra. "Why don't you cut that one?"

Petra took a step forwards, only to stop as something hard was pressed into the back of her neck.

"If I pull the trigger," Stefan said, "I will kill you, and your friend. Now, lower the gun, and take a seat on that chair over there. Stop," he said, as Petra started walking. "Put your gun on that table, and *then* walk over to the chair." Stefan waited for Petra to sit down, and then picked up the gun, stuffing it into his waistband as he beckoned for Berndt to come in.

"I hope you have good news, Aleksander," Johnson said.

"Berndt has a call scheduled with his crazy daughter for one o'clock," Stefan said, and nodded for Berndt to place his phone on the table between Johnson and Maratse. "That's in seven minutes."

"Seven whole minutes, eh?" Johnson looked at Petra. "I might have managed that in my youth, but I have to admit that it takes a little longer these days. Perhaps later, darling, what do you say to that?"

"*Eeqqi,*" Maratse said.

"What did he say?" Johnson said, and leaned closer to Maratse.

"It means *no.*" Maratse lunged for Johnson's throat. His fingers caught around the American's shirt as he stepped back, tearing a flap of cotton and ripping a few buttons before Stefan smacked Maratse on the back of the head with the butt of his pistol.

"You see this?" Johnson said to Berndt, pushing

at Maratse's head with his knuckles. "This is what you hired."

"Maratse?"

"The one and only. Pathetic, eh?"

"Leave him alone," Petra shouted.

"Sit down, sweetheart, don't exert yourself, it looks like you've had quite a night already." Johnson waved at Stefan to lower his gun. "Unless you've got something to trade?"

"I have Dieter's hard drive," she said.

"Here?"

"Close."

"Of course," Johnson said. "But now I have to do more than get your boyfriend drunk to make you hand it over." He gripped the knife in his hand. Petra held her breath as he held the knife to Maratse's chin.

"Wait," Berndt said, as his phone rang. He swiped the screen, and turned the phone on the speaker setting, dialling up the volume as Johnson lowered the knife.

"Daddy?"

Maratse recognised Therese Kleinschmidt's voice, but the shriek of wind in the background, and the crash of what sounded like waves, made it difficult to hear her.

"Therese, where are you?"

"I'm not going to make it. I'm sorry."

"What are you saying?" Berndt cast a wild glance at Johnson at the sound of something heavy cracking in the background.

"The mast?" Johnson said, with a shrug.

"Therese?"

"I'm sorry, Daddy."

Petra sat up as Johnson walked to the table and spun the phone towards him with his finger.

"Do you have the journal?" Johnson waited a beat. "Therese? The journal?"

"I always loved you, Daddy, like you were my own father."

Berndt pushed Johnson away from the phone and placed his hands either side of it. He leaned over the table, and said, "You should have been my daughter. You were the bravest…"

"Oh please," Johnson said. He pushed Berndt to one side, and shouted at the phone. "Kleinschmidt. Do you have the damn journal? Have you read it?"

"Yes," Therese said, her voice barely audible above the waves crashing over the *Ophelia*'s stricken hull.

"Have it or read it?"

"Read it."

"Finally," Johnson said. He tapped the tip of the knife on the table. "Tell me about thorium. Is that Wegener's secret? Is that what he found in the mountains?" Johnson placed his palms on the table and pressed his face towards the phone. "Come on, Therese. Daddy is waiting."

Johnson frowned, recoiling at a violent crash of static through the speaker, and the sound of something groaning, tipping, as if the *Ophelia* was rolling into the massive jaws of Greenland's dark seas.

"You're not my daddy," Therese said, and nothing more. The line went dead.

Johnson lifted the knife in his fist, raised it above his head, and curled it down in an arc towards the iPhone, just as Berndt collapsed onto his knees, and the windows of the restaurant imploded with a bang, and the flash and flare of magnesium.

The first GSG 9 officer to crash through the blinds and glass of the window put two bullets through Stefan's chest, and a third through his forehead. Two more officers slammed Johnson into the floor. One of them knelt on the American's chest, while his partner cinched plastic ties around his wrists. A fourth man covered Berndt while the fifth and sixth members of the team secured Maratse and Petra, dragging them out of the restaurant to the ambulances parked behind the police cordon at the end of the street. Hannah took Petra's hand and helped her into the ambulance.

"You're all right?"

"Yes."

Hannah moved to one side as the paramedics lowered Maratse onto a stretcher. He smiled at her, and said, "Don't mind the smell; I've had a bit to drink."

Petra waited for the medic to finish strapping Maratse to the stretcher, and then leaned over to brush a tear from his cheek with a dusty finger.

"Funny guy," she said, and smiled.

"Piitalaat."

"Yes?"

"I'm ready to go home."

"Yes. Let's do that." Petra waited as Maratse turned his head to one side and coughed; when he looked back he whispered her name. "What?"

"Don't eat my peanuts."

"Right," Petra said, as Hannah tapped her on the shoulder.

"You took a big risk," she said, "running away like that."

"I didn't run away." Petra opened the front of her vest and pulled out the hard drive. "I knew you would find me."

"The GPS tracker could have been damaged in

the blast."

Petra shrugged. "It wasn't." She turned at the sound of Johnson's voice as the GSG 9 team marched him towards the police car parked behind the assault vehicle. Berndt followed, flanked by two more GSG 9 men. "What happens to them?"

"Berndt's easy. With the evidence on the hard drive, and the testimony of the captain of the *Ophelia*, we can charge him with obstruction of justice at the very least, possibly conspiracy to…" Hannah paused at the sound of a vehicle braking hard outside the police cordon. She glanced at Petra, and took a step towards the car at the sound of two doors opening, shouts from police officers in German, and a loud male voice with an American accent.

"Who the hell's in charge here?"

"I am," Hannah said, as she took a step towards the tall man flashing a badge at her colleagues. Petra followed a step behind her.

"Your name?"

"Hannah Mayer."

"And you're in charge?"

"Yes. Who are you?"

"Who I am is above your pay grade. Now, here's what you are going to do." The man pulled out his phone and dialled a number. He held up a finger as Hannah started to speak. "Yes, sir, here she is now." He gave the phone to Hannah.

Petra watched as the man pulled Johnson away from the GSG 9 team holding him, and waited for Hannah to finish talking on his phone. Johnson caught Petra's eye and took a step towards her, nodding for her to join him.

"You see what's happening here, don't you, Sergeant?" Johnson said.

"I see you're still cuffed," she said, with a glance at the plastic ties around his wrists.

"An oversight."

"Really?"

"Of course," he said, "but in the meantime, now that we have a moment, and your boyfriend is otherwise engaged, how about you ask me the question."

Petra looked over her shoulder at Maratse. She caught his eye and smiled.

"Hurry now, Sergeant."

Petra lifted her chin and looked Johnson in the eye. "You're CIA."

"Am I?"

"Nele was working for you. She said so."

"She didn't say my name."

"She didn't need to."

"So ask the question, *Piitalaat*." Johnson grinned. "I'm a quick study."

"Why?"

"You're gonna go with *why*?"

"Yes."

Johnson glanced at Hannah, frowning at the curl of her lips. "I'll tell you why," he said, and looked at Petra. "Because oil is running out, and Greenland has no viable oil. But what you do have is two handfuls of people on a frozen rock in the middle of the Atlantic, with no connecting roads, and a national desire for independence. You want to be free of Denmark, and I can make that happen."

"One mine at a time?"

"Why not?"

"I'll tell you why not," Petra said, and took a step closer to Johnson. "Because while you win the hearts of one handful with your promise of money, you'll be poisoning the minds of the other by dumping waste from the mines into the water. We've been down that road already. People like you promise jobs for Greenlanders, and then claim we don't have the qualifications. You promise the government huge payouts once your overheads have been met, but neglect to tell them it will take thirty years or more for a tiny percentage of the profits. It's been done before."

"And it will be done again, Sergeant. Don't you want to know why?"

"Because we're a bunch of ignorant and uncultured Eskimos?"

"I was going to say *natives*, but I'll go with Eskimos. Anyway," Johnson said, as he held out his wrists, "I think I'll be going now. This conversation is getting boring."

Petra took a step back as the American in the suit pulled a pair of metal handcuffs from his belt and slapped them around Johnson's wrists.

"What the hell?"

"Sam Johnson?"

"Yes?"

"I have been authorised to detain you for questioning in regard to matters concerning espionage, conspiracy, and," the man paused, "insider trading. It seems you own a mining company Mr Johnson, and they appear to have gone bust."

"I don't own a mining company."

"We'll let the lawyers deal with the specifics, but, as of today, you do. The Greenlandic part, anyway."

"What the hell?" Johnson looked at his watch. "It's past midnight, for God's sake. I told them not to sign if they didn't hear from me by the end of the day."

Petra leaned forwards, and said, "We're four

hours behind in Greenland. How's that for ignorant?"

Petra smiled all the way to the ambulance, climbed up the steps and sat down on the seat beside Maratse. She took his hand and kissed him on the cheek as the paramedic adjusted the saline drip and the driver closed the doors.

"We're going home," she said.

Chapter 22

The commissioner called it extended leave and the police union agreed, provided that Petra receive the proper psychological support following an extensive debrief. It should have happened in Greenland, but, given her German language skills, a generous licence was applied and the union accepted the assistance of the Bundespolizei, with a representative from the Danish police sitting in on the different meetings. The debrief took three days, and Maratse met Petra at the same café at the foot of the television tower in *Alexanderplatz* at the same time each day. Petra translated the articles in *Die Welt* and *Berliner Zeitung* while Maratse fiddled with the tubes of sugar, watched the crowds and looked at Petra. He lost interest in the story once Petra confirmed that Dieter was fit to fly, and he and the captain of the *Ophelia* were being escorted out of Greenland in the custody of the German Bundespolizei, after negotiations at the political level. Petra read about Berndt and a shadowy figure referred to as an American. She started to read the articles mentioning the two Greenlanders involved in the police operations in the city, only to stop, and look up when Maratse placed his finger on the paper.

"Don't bother with that one," he said, "I know what happened in the restaurant."

"I'm sorry."

"Don't be." He tapped an article next to the account of the storming of the restaurant. "Read that one."

Petra frowned, and said, "It's about a political scandal. Unrelated."

"Read it anyway,"

"You're sure?"

"*Iiji.*"

Petra started to read, curling her hair behind her ear, and tracing her finger beneath the words in the article. She tapped the page each time a particular word challenged her, as she searched for the Danish translation of more specific terms. When she had to pause for a fourth time, she stopped, her gaze focussed on the paper, and said, "I know what you're doing." She bit at the smile quivering on her bottom lip.

"I'm listening."

"Okay," she said, and looked up. "What's it about?"

"I'm not listening to the words, Piitalaat."

"I know."

Petra pressed her hand on top of Maratse's, brushing her fingers across the tiny fishing scars, the nicks and cuts in his nails.

"I don't know what this is," she said.

"Neither do I."

"Maybe it's the trauma, shared experiences, something." Petra looked up. "But I feel safe with you. I can be myself."

"Thirteen years, Piitalaat."

"I don't care about that," she said, and squeezed his hand. "You hear about it all the time."

"Famous people, maybe."

"Not just famous people. We both know lots of couples in Greenland, with a bigger age gap than ours."

Maratse smiled, and said, "The man is usually

better looking."

"You worry about that?" Petra let go of Maratse's hand, and placed hers over her mouth, suppressing a giggle. Her eyes danced, the red and green Christmas lights flickering in her deep-brown irises. Petra's shoulders twitched, and she said, "Really?"

"Maybe," he said. "Sometimes."

Petra wiped a tear from her eye, folded the newspapers onto the table, and stood up. "Come on," she said, and held out her hand.

The Berlin Christmas markets were crowded, and Maratse let Petra lead him by the hand between the stalls, through the maze of ornaments, past seasonal aromas – candied and curried spices. They ate *currywurst* from paper trays with wooden forks, shared a beer, and spent their last night in Berlin in the same hotel room, his arm curled around her slim, warm body, her hair tickling his nose.

"I still don't know," Petra whispered.

"Neither do I."

It took a day to fly from Berlin to Copenhagen, to Kangerlussuaq, to Ilulissat, to Qaarsut. Karl met them outside the airport, and they got a lift down to the ice in the yellow-and-red-striped airport Land Cruiser. He fiddled with the sledge as Petra changed into her salopettes, zipped her jacket to just below her chin, and tugged a thick fleece hat over her long black hair.

"We're taking the dogs," Karl said. "You can't get three on a snowmobile."

"Any peanuts?" Maratse asked, with a look at Petra.

"What?"

"Don't mind him," Petra said. "He just doesn't understand the rules of flying."

"There are rules?" Karl said.

"Yes. Petra gets the peanuts," she said.

Karl looked at them and shook his head. "Come on. Let's go home."

The open leads of black water had stretched since they had last travelled across the ice, and Karl swung the team away from the coast before curving in a long arc to the beach of Inussuk. Petra leaned into Maratse's arms as the frost coated the tips of her hair in brittle white sleeves. Maratse relaxed as Karl drove the team with soft claps of his hands, and the occasional snap of the whip on the ice.

Buuti met them on the ice, together with Edvard and his wife, Nukannguaq. Maratse smiled as the two women enveloped Petra with soft shrieks and warm hugs, tugging her away to the house as the men unsnapped the dogs from the team, secured them to the ice and fed them. Maratse shook Edvard's hand, frowning as the women shrieked again on the deck of Buuti's house.

"It's Nukannguaq," Edvard said. "She's pregnant."

"Congratulations," Maratse said, and slapped Edvard on the back.

"We're pleased," he said, and nodded at Karl. "What about you?"

"Me?"

"You and Petra?"

Karl crunched through the snow and shook his head. "Don't ask, Edvard. It has something to do with peanuts."

"Peanuts?"

"Come on," Karl said, and pointed at the house. "Let's eat."

The houses of Inussuk glittered with paper stars. They filled the windows, hanging from electrical cords, lit with soft bulbs. The lights were turned on the first night of Advent, and would stay lit until Christmas was past, and the sun had turned, creeping towards the horizon. There were two stars hanging in the windows of Maratse's house, and he thanked Karl as they clumped up the stairs after the women.

"Thank Buuti," he said.

The windows steamed as they ate into the night, laughing at stories shared around the table, tales of the hunt, the condition of the ice. Maratse caught Petra's eye at the end of the table, watched as she teased at a strand of hair hanging over her cheek, smiling as Nukannguaq filled Petra's glass with more wine. They didn't talk, just looked, until the meal was over, the stories had been repeated twice, maybe three times, and it was time to leave.

"I'll sleep on the sofa," Maratse said, as they hung their jackets in the hall.

"No," Petra whispered. She took his hand, bit at her bottom lip and then led him upstairs.

Maratse found a note beside the bed in the morning. He squinted as he read it, curling his head on the pillow, breathing in the last of Petra's perfume, before he slipped out of bed, and clumped down the stairs. He ignored the familiar ache in his legs, made coffee, and smiled at the thought of Petra sledging into Uummannaq with Karl to do some shopping. She would stay for Christmas, the note said.

Maratse sipped his coffee by the window, his face lit in the soft glow of the paper star. He tugged at his t-shirt, and waved at Buuti as she climbed the steps to his house, kicked the snow from her boots, and opened the door.

"Hi," Maratse said. "Coffee?"

"*Naamik*," Buuti said. She waited by the door.

"You're not coming in?"

She shook her head. "Karl called."

"*Iiji*?"

"He said your mobile is off."

Maratse nodded. "Battery needs charging. What is it?"

"He's ready to leave Uummannaq, but he can't find Petra. She's not answering her mobile."

"It's here," Maratse said, and pointed at the two phones charging on the windowsill.

"Okay, but Karl needs to come back. He told his sister to look out for Petra."

"I can pick her up."

"Sure." Buuti nodded. She turned to leave, and then stopped. "We're happy for you, David."

"*Qujanaq*." Maratse smiled as Buuti shut the door.

He tapped the screens of the phones on the windowsill, and then walked to the kitchen. Maratse boiled more water, made fresh coffee, opened the fridge only to shake his head and close it again. Karl had fed his dogs while he was away, but the cupboards were bare. If Petra had her phone, he realised, he could ask her to buy some food – potatoes, before the store ran out.

Maratse closed the fridge as the landline rang. Coffee dribbled out of the machine and spat on the hotplate warming the glass, as Maratse walked around the sofa to answer the phone. He picked it up, smiling at Petra's scent locked into his t-shirt.

"Maratse?"

"*Iiji*."

"It's Aqqa Danielsen. Simonsen needs you to come into town."

"Why?"

Danielsen waited a beat, and then said, "I can't really say. It's best you come."

"What's going on, Aqqa?"

"It's Sergeant Jensen…"

"*Iiji?*"

"We think she's been taken."

The End

Author's Note

Greenland is the largest island in the world, but with roughly 56,000 inhabitants, its population could squeeze in to Dodger Stadium in Los Angeles, California, USA. The capital of Nuuk has a population of roughly 15,000 people. Some settlements have fewer than one hundred residents. There are no roads connecting the towns, villages, and settlements. Transport to and from the inhabited areas is predominantly serviced by planes with short take off and landing capabilities, helicopters, and boats. In the areas where the sea ice is thick enough, Greenlanders can travel across the ice in cars, and by snow scooters and dog sledges.

Constable David Maratse's fictive Greenland is affected by the same limitations of the real Greenland. His fictive stories are inspired by some events and many places that exist in Greenland. Most place names are the same, such as Nuuk, and Uummannaq, but used fictitiously. The settlement of Inussuk does not exist, although observant readers looking at a map will be able to take a good guess at where it might be found.

The storyline surrounding Alfred Wegener's journal and his discovery in Svartenhuk, is also, purely fictitious.

Chris
May 2018
Denmark

Acknowledgments

I would like to thank Isabel Dennis-Muir for her invaluable editing skills and feedback on the manuscript, and to Julia Yeates for her generous proof-reading. While several people have contributed to Blood Floe, the mistakes and inaccuracies are all my own.

Chris
May 2018
Denmark

About the Author

Christoffer Petersen is the pen name for an author living in Denmark. Chris started writing stories about Greenland while teaching in Qaanaaq, the largest village in the very north of Greenland – the population peaked at 600 during the two years he lived there. He spent a total of seven years in Greenland.

Chris continues to be inspired by the vast icy wilderness of the Arctic and his books have a common setting in the region, with a Scandinavian influence. He has also watched enough Bourne movies to no longer be surprised by the plot, but not enough to get bored.

You can find Chris in Denmark or online here:

www.christoffer-petersen.com

By the same Author

THE GREENLAND CRIME SERIES
featuring Constable David Maratse

SEVEN GRAVES, ONE WINTER Book 1
BLOOD FLOE Book 2
WE SHALL BE MONSTERS Book 3
INSIDE THE BEAR'S CAGE Book 4
WHALE HEART Book 5

Novellas from the same series

KATABATIC #1
CONTAINER #2
TUPILAQ #3
THE LAST FLIGHT #4
THE HEART THAT WAS A WILD GARDEN #5
QIVITTOQ #6
THE THUNDER SPIRITS #7
ILULIAQ #8
SCRIMSHAW #9
ASIAQ #10
CAMP CENTURY #11
INUK #12
DARK CHRISTMAS #13
POISON BERRY #14
NORTHERN MAIL #15
SIKU #16
VIRUSI #17

BAIT #18
THE WOMEN'S KNIFE #19
ICE, WIND & FIRE #20

Omnibus editions of the Short Stories

THE GREENLAND TRILOGY
featuring Konstabel Fenna Brongaard

THE ICE STAR Book 1
IN THE SHADOW OF THE MOUNTAIN Book 2
THE SHAMAN'S HOUSE Book 3

THE POLARPOL ACTION THRILLERS
featuring Sergeant Petra Jensen and more

NORTHERN LIGHT Book 1
MOUNTAIN GHOST Book 2

THE DETECTIVE FREJA HANSEN SERIES
set in Denmark and Scotland

FELL RUNNER Introductory novella
BLACKOUT INGÉNUE Book 1

THE WILD CRIME SERIES
set in Denmark, Alaska and Ukraine

PAINT THE DEVIL Book 1

LOST IN THE WOODS Book 2
CHERNOBYL WOLVES Book 3

MADE IN DENMARK
short stories *featuring* Milla Moth set in Denmark

DANISH DESIGN Story 1

THE WHEELMAN SHORTS
short stories *featuring* Noah Lee set in Australia

PULP DRIVER Story 1

THE DARK ADVENT SERIES
featuring Police Commissioner Petra "Piitalaat"
Jensen set in Greenland

THE CALENDAR MAN Book 1
THE TWELFTH NIGHT Book 2
INVISIBLE TOUCH Book 3
NORTH STAR BAY Book 4

GREENLAND NOIR POETRY
with characters from the Greenland Crime Series
GREENLAND NOIR Volume 1

UNDERCOVER GREENLAND
featuring Eko Simigaq and Inniki Rasmussen

NARKOTIKA Book 1

CAPTAIN ERRONEOUS SMITH
featuring Captain Erroneous Smith

THE ICE CIRCUS Book 1

THE BOLIVIAN GIRL
a hard-hitting military and political thriller series

THE BOLIVIAN GIRL Book 1

GUERRILLA GREENLAND
featuring Constable David Maratse

ARCTIC STATE Novella 1
ARCTIC REBEL Novella 2

OUTBACK NOIR
featuring Detective Braidyn Clancy

CROCODILE BEAT Book 1

THE WESTERNS
featuring Captain Constantine

BEYOND THE RANGES Collection 1